NOBLE INTENT
RAPTUROUS INTENT ROCKSTARS
BOOK 1

CADENCE KEYS

Copyright © 2022 by Cadence Keys

All rights reserved.

No part of this book may be reproduced in any form or by any electronic or mechanical means, including information storage and retrieval systems, without written permission from the author, except for the use of brief quotations in a book review.

This book is a work of fiction. Names, characters, places, and incidents are a product of the author's imagination. Locales and public names are sometimes used for atmospheric purposes. Any resemblances to actual people, living or dead, businesses, companies, events, institutions, or locales are entirely coincidental. Any trademarks, service marks, product names, or named features are assumed to be the property of their respective owners and are used only for reference.

Editors: Happily Editing Anns

Cover Design: Lily Bear Design Co

For my dad, who may not have been the man who gave me his DNA, but who showed me what a father's love really looked like. Thank you for always making sure I knew I was enough.
I love you.

1

TRENT

The crowd gathered around my SUV erupts in cheers as I exit from the backseat, my bodyguard already standing by my door. My smile is pasted on my face, and I'm thankful for the sunglasses that hide the dissatisfaction in my eyes at the scene in front of me. The screams from the women being held back by security are nearly deafening as my bodyguard helps guide me safely inside the popular downtown building where I'll be having my magazine interview and photoshoot today.

Simone Jacobs, the journalist who's interviewing me today, meets me inside, a coy smile on her face. "Mr. Bridger, it's so great to finally meet you. Sorry for all the craziness out there."

"How'd they know I'd be here?"

She's trained well because her face only freezes for a second before she gives the standard line of bullshit claiming there was some internal memo that accidentally got out. We both know the truth. They wanted extra publicity and they got it. That's why I'm here after all. For the publicity.

Some days that's all my life feels like—some publicity stunt.

Don't get me wrong, I love my job. But more and more it feels like just that—a job—instead of the dream come true that it used to be.

Being a famous rock star isn't all it is cut out to be. There are perks, sure, but no one tells you about the rest of it. The fact that you can never go anywhere in public without being recognized—and subsequently swarmed—by people wanting something from you, or worse, touching you without your permission. You're no longer a person to them, you're an ideal. You're their chance to be close to fame.

I remember the feeling well. I remember the first time I met my idol backstage at a concert when we opened for his band. I thought I'd died and gone to heaven. I couldn't understand the jaded look in his eyes at the time, but I get it now.

Some days I wish I could go back to being that naive Texas boy who thought hitting it big was going to change my life for the better. It changed my life, but I don't know if I'm better off than I was when I was broke and couch surfing with friends as we'd hop from town to town playing in dive bars. Back when people cared who I was as a person and not just a rock star.

Simone walks us down a hall and then we're in a large open room with a couch and some chairs set up in one corner and camera equipment and wardrobe options taking up the rest of the space. I know at least one of our shots will be on the roof with the backdrop of LA behind me; that's why they picked this specific building to begin with.

She leads us straight to the couch and chairs and gestures for me to choose where I'd like to sit. I elect a chair, preferring the comfort of knowing she can't sit right next to me. I've had a few journalists try to cross that professional boundary, and while I might have considered it when I was younger and still new to this lifestyle, it's not something I'm interested in now.

Meaningless fucks lost their appeal a long time ago.

She's still starry-eyed when she sits down and gushes about how she's such a big fan. I dig deep—deeper than I usually have to—to get into character. To become the Trent Bridger she expects. The only version of Trent Bridger most people expect these days.

"So, I've been wondering this since you guys broke out on the scene a few years ago and blew up. How'd you come up with your band name, Rapturous Intent?"

I offer her my most charming smile. "It means that we expect the women we're with to experience rapture when they come. The kind of blinding pleasure that's so intense, they forget their own name."

Her eyes widen, and she nibbles her lip before clearing her throat. "I have no doubt you deliver. So, how did you guys meet? Tristan is your brother, but what about your drummer, Miles Tallon, and bass player, Kasen Stone?"

"Tristan is my younger brother, and we went to high school with Miles and Kasen. I first met them in band class my freshman year. Miles was a sophomore, and Tristan and I had been playing together and writing songs for a couple of years, but more as a hobby than anything serious. Then when Tristan finally came to our high school—Kasen and I were juniors—we decided to take it a little more seriously. We played local shows until Tristan graduated and then his best friend, Robbie Nolan, became our band manager and got us booked at a bunch of different smaller venues all over the country. We did tours like that for a year or two before we got the chance to open for a fairly popular band, and that kind of opened the door for us. We started getting more gigs and then got signed with our label, and the rest is history."

"And you and your brother are the main songwriters, correct?"

"Yep. We've been writing together since we were eleven and thirteen respectively. We've perfected our process over the years, and it hasn't let us down yet."

"No, it certainly hasn't. Your latest single has been number one on the charts for eight weeks straight. And your upcoming tour sold out in minutes. How does it feel to know you've become one of the most famous bands in history? I mean, people are comparing you to Foo Fighters."

My body warms at that comparison. It started with our last single and has been making the rounds in the press. It's probably the single greatest compliment I've ever been given in this industry because that band was definitely a huge influence on me growing up.

"It's a huge honor to be compared to people I admire so much, and it's a distinction I always dreamed of but never thought we'd actually achieve."

If only it made up for the empty feeling that comes whenever I leave the stage. The isolation I feel even when I'm in a crowd of people, and the unending loneliness when I realize I'll likely never find someone who truly wants to know *me*, the real me.

If such a woman exists, I've yet to find her.

Every woman I've dated in the past few years has ended up wanting some part of my fame—whether it was to make Hollywood connections or just to rub elbows with other rock stars. None of them have really cared about me for me. They just wanted to say they dated *the* Trent Bridger.

My stomach sours because I hate feeling ungrateful for this crazy wonderful life I live, filled with more luxury than I ever dreamed of. But more and more lately I miss the simplicity of my life before I was famous.

"Here's another one I'm dying to know." Her eyes spark mischievously. "What's the wildest thing that's ever happened on tour?"

I rub my chin like I have to think about which story to tell her. I can imagine what she thinks would be wild, but it's probably tame compared to some of the stories I could tell her. Like the time I showed up to my hotel room to find a naked groupie on my bed with rose petals and my name tattooed on her body. Or the time I walked into a popular coffee chain to grab a coffee after a long night recording in the studio and had a woman walk up to me and grope my dick through my jeans and proposition me. No, she probably wants some wild story about the band. But Kasen's a party boy, and I don't particularly want to get into his history of drug use. Tristan is a playboy, but only because he can't have the one woman he's actually in love with. And Miles...well, let's just say Miles has quite the adventurous sex life, which is something you'd never guess based on his normally chill, stoner-esque personality. That man likes it dirty.

But none of those stories are mine to tell.

So instead, I lean forward like I'm about to tell her the best secret of her life and whisper seductively, "What happens on the road, stays on the road, darlin'."

Her lips part and her breath quickens—just the reaction I was going for. I sit back in my chair, and it takes her a moment before she returns to her own upright position, her eyes still a little distant like she's imagining a lot of naughty things that might happen on the road.

She's probably not too far off from the truth.

She clears her throat again, clearly trying to regain her composure, but her husky voice gives her away when she speaks. "I've got just a few more questions, and then we'll move to your photoshoot."

My body already feels exhausted from having to maintain this persona and pretend like I'm into this whole interview, but this is what I signed up for.

If only someone had told me to read the fine print of becoming famous.

2

BECKA

The room erupts in applause as I stare in dismal shock. Everything feels like a blur as I watch Brad—the man I dated for nearly a year and thought I was going to marry—hold up Shelly's left hand for the whole room. Nearly everyone who works for VibeTV, the streaming service that's said to be the next Netflix, is present in the massive auditorium that the company uses to preview final cuts of upcoming releases and for big staff announcements. Today the announcement seems to be that Brad has ripped my heart out—the evidence being the insanely oversized rock of a diamond engagement ring sitting on Shelly's left hand.

I feel like I'm going to be sick.

But I can't look away. It's my own personal train wreck. I'm fighting back the urge to cover my face with my hands and peek between my fingers so I can still see what's going on, but I'm in such shock I can't move. My arms rest heavily against my side, my feet are glued to the floor, and my heart feels like it either fell like a stone into my stomach or disintegrated entirely—I can't quite tell.

It wasn't supposed to be like this. He said he wanted some

time apart to figure himself out. He told me he loved me but he wasn't the marrying kind.

And I'm the fool who fell for it. When will I ever learn that men are apparently nothing but liars?

He smiles down at Shelly and winks at her—fucking winks at her! I'm the one he used to wink at. He used to save all those sultry, happy smiles for me. What the fuck is even happening? My utter heartbreak and betrayal quickly morph into anger. I can't believe he didn't even have the decency to give me a heads-up. Everyone knows that we were together for nine months. He's only been with Shelly for like two fricking seconds!

Okay, so it's been a month, but still. What the actual fuck? I knew I never should've caved. I had rules against dating guys I worked with for a reason, but Brad was so convincing. He spent months pursuing me relentlessly before I even agreed to go out with him, making me feel special and telling me over and over again that he really felt like we were kindred spirits meant to be together.

What a load of horseshit.

I can feel my emotions rollercoastering around my body—one minute furious, the next devastated. Tears burn at the back of my eyes, but I refuse to cry in front of my coworkers. I'm not that girl. Hell, I rarely cry at all.

I watch Brad and Shelly smile at everyone in our office. Shelly's curly blonde hair and saccharine grin make me want to scream and rage, but instead I continue to stand here, watching, waiting for someone to tell me this is some big cosmic joke.

This is not happening.

I can't believe this is happening.

I'm suddenly grateful I never told my brother about Brad because I'm certain he'd kill him if he knew. Will has always been protective of me. We're only eleven months apart in age, and after our dad left when I was four, he took over the job of protecting me, our older sister, Lainey, and younger sister, Elise. In the past few years, I've grown more hesitant about letting the guys I date meet my brother, partly because he can be so overprotective, but also because the guys I've dated have been one giant disappointment after another.

By the time I was ready to introduce Brad to Will, things had started to feel off. Brad was pulling away and working more and more, and then suddenly he was saying he needed a little break to get his head sorted. Clearly he sorted his head right up Shelly's ass.

As people around me move closer toward the happy couple—barf—I feel my body finally loosen up and quickly hightail it out of there. No way will I be congratulating them.

Not today.

I'll be a bigger person later, but today I'm going to be small and miserable. Pushing past the dozens of coworkers swarming around trying to congratulate Brad and Shelly, I manage to make it outside our office building in Santa Monica barely holding onto my sanity. How the fuck could Brad blindside me like this? If he had no intention of us ever getting back together, why has he been stringing me along since he broke up with me two months ago?

My heart aches at the idea that he was laughing at me behind my back—like I was some joke. *Oh, look at how I can keep the foolish woman on my line like a fish with bait.* Every warning sign and red flag comes flashing back to me as I replay the nine months we were together and the six months before that when he was wooing me. He pursued me with a tenacity that I'd never experienced from a man before.

After a while it became impossible to resist. And while I'm not a fan of becoming office gossip, it was hard to keep an office romance like ours a secret after how open he'd been in his pursuit of me. And it was refreshing to be with a guy so put-together after dating a bunch of losers who would always conveniently "forget" their wallets when we were out to dinner. Or who found ways to undermine my intelligence in nearly microscopic ways that left me feeling small and insignificant by the time they were finished with me.

I hang my head in shame because it has become painfully obvious that Brad is really no different than any of those guys. I was played. It's that simple. Once again a man has let me down. Story of my fucking life. It started with my deadbeat dad peacing out when I was four and has been a recurring theme in my life. What is it about me that makes men treat me like I'm disposable?

Needing more time before I go back to the office, I decide to take an impromptu walk to the promenade. It won't be busy this time of day, and it's away from the disgustingly happy couple so that's what counts.

I'm lost in my thoughts, remembering all the tender caresses and the hundreds of times Brad told me if he was the marrying kind, I would be the woman he would choose. I shake my head in frustration, the tears officially falling down my face now, which only angers me more. Even if I know it's stupid to cry over him, I can't fight the hurt. Why am I never good enough? Why won't anyone ever stay for me? Fight for me? Tears cascade faster down my face, and I start to notice people gawking at me as they walk past.

Wonderful. Now I'm the sad, pathetic woman who is crying on a sidewalk in public.

Could this day get any worse?

No sooner do I think the words than I bump into a tall figure exiting the building next to me.

"Oh my gosh, I'm so sorry," I say, the words coming out a little muffled and cracked from the emotion clogging my throat and streaming down my face.

"Becks?"

I vaguely recognize the voice, but it can't be who I think it is. It can't.

I look up into the familiar ocean-blue eyes of Trent Bridger, the lead singer of Rapturous Intent—the hottest band on the charts—my brother's oldest friend, and the first boy I ever kissed.

So apparently this day can get worse.

3

TRENT

My gaze slides over Becka Edmonson's face, and I can feel the pull of the frown on my own at the sight of her tears.

"Becks? What's wrong?"

I hate her tears, but it doesn't diminish her beauty in the slightest. She's just as gorgeous as always. Her coffee-brown hair spills over her shoulders and down just past her breasts, the lighter hues catching the light of the sun and making her hair look even more shiny and smooth than I remember it. Her curves seem fuller than they used to be, but she still looks trim and could easily pass for a model, not that she'd ever realize that. Becka never understood how beautiful she is, even when I'd watch the boys at school practically fall all over themselves for her attention.

She shakes her head and lets out a shuddering breath, wiping her nose on the sleeve of her shirt at the same time. She stares up at the sky and I swear I hear her mumbling "seriously" under her breath.

"Becka?" I prod, hoping she'll finally answer me. She couldn't possibly forget who I am. We grew up together, and her brother is still my friend. Hell, at one time she and I were great friends too. Will, Becks, and I used to get into all kinds of trouble growing up, riding our bikes through the neighborhood well into the nighttime hours, staying up late to catch fireflies, and when we were older sneaking out to steal sips of Tony Ramirez's dad's liquor.

She was even my first kiss, not that it was a great one for either of us. I'll begrudgingly admit I had no idea what I was doing, and it was a lot more slobbery than it should've been. But that's not what caused us to hang out less. At least I never attributed our faded friendship to that one kiss. It always just seemed like we went our own directions. But seeing her now takes me back once again to all those memories of the days before I was famous.

Her jade-green eyes are mesmerizing and heartbreaking at the same time. "Nothing. I'm fine. What are you doing here? I thought you'd be on tour already."

My pulse speeds up in excitement that she's followed my band. She knows I have an upcoming tour. I'm ashamed to admit I have no idea what she's up to these days, but that's beside the point.

"Nice deflection, but you forget I know you." It's been years since I've seen her, but that doesn't change the fact that I knew her nearly as well as I know her brother Will. I arch my brow, daring her to argue with me. "Now tell me what's wrong."

She gestures behind me. "Were you going somewhere? I don't want to hold you up." I glance back to see what she's looking at and realize she's staring at my behemoth of a bodyguard.

"Oh, that's just Chris, my bodyguard. Don't worry about him."

She stares at me like she wants to say something else, but instead her shoulders sag in defeat, and she gestures to the coffee shop I just walked out of. "Let's at least sit. It's been a long day, and I could really use a cup of coffee." I open the door for her and follow her to a table in the back, while Chris sits at the table in front of us, his eyes cataloging every person in the room.

Becka watches him cautiously before turning to me. "Does he go with you everywhere?"

"Yep, pretty much. Definitely any time I'm in public. There

was an incident about a year ago that got out of hand, and the rest of the band felt it safest if I had some kind of protection."

"Do all the guys have bodyguards?"

"Not as regularly as I do. Being the lead singer brings with it a certain level of fame that none of us were prepared for. We always have extra security when we're all together, but I'm the only one who regularly needs someone with me."

Her eyes turn sad as she glances back at Chris and then locks her gaze with mine. "That doesn't exactly seem like a dream come true."

I shrug. "It comes with the territory. Anyway, stop deflecting and tell me what's wrong."

She sighs heavily and then says, "How about you tell me what you're doing here and then I'll tell you why I'm upset."

I squint at her, wondering if she's just trying to get out of telling me what's going on, but decide to play along since at least she admitted she's upset.

"I had a meeting with VibeTV. They bought the rights to a documentary on the band that we'll be filming during our upcoming tour. I just signed the contract this morning with the guys, and then decided to stop for tea before heading home."

Becka's face lights up. "First of all, congrats, that's awesome, and second,"—her eyes get a mischievous little twinkle and my heart speeds up infinitesimally—"I can't wait to work with you."

My jaw drops. "What?"

She lets out a soft laugh, and I'm relieved to see her face lose the pain that was there when we first bumped into each other. "I work in the PR department for VibeTV. I've been there for three years now. If you just signed the contract today, my boss will probably announce it to the team tomorrow. So, thanks for giving me the inside scoop. It almost makes up for this craptastic day."

"Yeah, about that…I think it's your turn to share."

"Ugh, do I have to?"

I smirk. "'Fraid so. We had a deal."

She looks down at her hands clasped together resting on the table, shakes her head, and then looks back up at me and tells me all about her—as she put it—craptastic day. Hearing how her ex treated her sends a fiery rage storming through my body. Even I know it's an extreme reaction for someone I haven't seen in years, but it takes me by such surprise there's no way of stopping it. She doesn't cry anymore, but her lip wobbles every so often, especially when she seems to be putting herself down. If I have to hear her call herself stupid one more time, I'm gonna shut that shit down.

Becka Edmonson is the smartest, kindest, funniest, bravest woman I've ever met. And I've met a lot of women. But she's always been at the top when it comes to women I admire.

I didn't realize how much I missed having her in my life until now, even if we are discussing a man who clearly didn't deserve her. I'm suddenly beyond grateful that we bumped into each other. I've always considered Becka a good friend, even if there was a time in my life where I wanted her to be more.

Sitting here with her is giving me something I haven't felt in a long-ass time. The exact thing I've been craving. She's not hanging out with me for my money or my fame. She's not trying to get in my pants—not that I'd stop her if she was. But more than any of that, she knows me, like really *knows* me.

It's beyond refreshing to sit across from someone who knew me before, someone I know would never use me for my fame because that's never been who she is. Becka's never been a people user. If anything, she lets others take from her until she's running on fumes, while she never takes back. The more she talks about Brad, the more I realize she still hasn't found the guy who will give to her, who will fill her cup endlessly so she never questions his love or her value in his life.

That's the type of man she needs. Not these douchebags she's always been drawn to.

"Yeah, so that's why I'm bawling in the middle of the day on a Wednesday—because I have terrible taste in men." She glances behind me and points. "That's probably the kind of guy I should be dating."

I turn around to see who she's pointing at. He's tall, dark-haired, and dressed in a tailored suit, but he also reeks of pompous douchebag.

"That is most definitely *not* the kind of guy you should be dating."

Her jaw drops, and her eyes look at me with dismay. "What do you mean? He clearly has a job and makes decent money, so he wouldn't mooch off of me. And he's attractive in a classic kind of way."

"That guy is a total player and would be a complete waste of your time."

"How do you figure? You only took one look at him."

"Yeah, and his eyes never strayed from looking at the barista's tits. Not to mention the faint line where a wedding band is either supposed to be or was, which tells me he's either a cheater or recently divorced and on the rebound. Just because a man wears a tailored suit doesn't mean he's not a total and complete asshole. Looks can be deceiving."

She watches the guy carefully, and I can practically see the gears in her head turning over my comments as she reevaluates him.

"Well, shit," she says, leaning back in her chair and looking at me with a mix of awe and disappointment.

"Sorry, Becks. You need better guy-dar."

She watches me thoughtfully. "Or maybe I just need you to help me pick out the next guy I date."

Wait, what?

"You don't go on tour for a few weeks, right?"

"A little over a month, yeah."

She smiles, and if I wasn't so taken aback by what she's suggesting, I'd be completely dazzled by her. "Great. Then you can be my dating coach."

"Your what now?"

"You heard me." She leans forward, her smile wide and her eyes bright with eagerness, while she points to where the suited guy was standing. Her eyes never leave mine. "You were able to tell from one glance that Mr. Tall, Dark, and Handsome was a hot mess express. That's what I need. We'll hang out like the old days, and you can help me pick out a guy who doesn't totally suck, because I'm so fucking tired of dating assholes. Trent, please save me from the assholes."

She holds her hands in front of her like she's praying and pleads with her intense green eyes.

I admit it; I'm not entirely opposed to the idea, mainly because it would give me an excuse to hang out with her. And after the past few months of feeling like I'm faking it for everyone else, it would be nice to be able to just be myself with someone, without any hidden agendas.

And Becka clearly does need a dating coach. So, why shouldn't it be me?

"Fine. You're on. What are you doing Friday?"

She smiles that breathtaking smile again, and I swear her eyes twinkle. "You tell me."

"Ian's in Hollywood. This Friday, seven o'clock. It's trivia night and there's always a ton of single guys there. I bet we can find you one there."

"Alright, Obi-wan. You're my only hope, so let's do this."

4

Becka

They say first impressions are everything. I'm not sure who *they* are exactly, but I've always lived by this saying and tonight is no different. I look at my reflection in the mirror and feel my confidence rise, even if there's still a part of me that's nervous about tonight.

I'm dressed in tight skinny jeans that show off my ass, my go-to ruby-red stilettos which are not only ridiculously comfortable for stilettos, but also incredibly fashionable with pretty much any outfit, a tight red tank top that hints at my cleavage without sending a *come and get it* message, and my favorite worn black leather jacket. I grab my clutch and head out to meet my Uber at the curb.

I've spent the last two days questioning my sanity. How could I have asked—okay, practically begged—Trent to be my dating coach?!

Trent of all people.

The same Trent I grew up with. The guy who was my brother's best friend growing up, even when they had completely different interests. If someone had told me a week ago that I'd ask Trent Bridger to be my dating coach, I would've laughed in their face and then promptly flipped them off. I've already decided that

I had momentary insanity when I suggested the idea to Trent. The more I've thought about it over the past couple of days, the more I realized the last thing I need right now is to be dating at all. I need some me time to reevaluate what I really want in a partner—and to make sure I don't settle for less than what I deserve the next time I decide to date a guy.

But instead of bailing on tonight, I decided to still meet up with Trent because it'll be nice just to spend some time with him and see how he's changed over the years. I know he still talks to Will, but it's been years since he and I have seen each other. And it's been even longer since I've been back to our old neighborhood. That feels like someone else's life sometimes. We've all come so far since those days—Will's now a famous pro football player, and Trent is getting panties tossed at him while he performs on world famous stages.

And yet, he still seemed like the down-to-earth guy he's always been when we hung out at the coffee shop. I hope he is still that guy, and that it wasn't just a fluke. It'll be awkward if he turns out to be an asshole himself, since my boss announced yesterday that I'm going to be the point person for all the PR for the Rapturous Intent documentary.

I slide out of my Uber in front of the trendy bar in Hollywood. It's clear the city is trying to clean up this stretch of Hollywood, but the faint scent of urine that seems like a fixture of this area still permeates the air.

The door opens to a platform with a set of stairs on the left going up and another set on the right going down. A sign in the middle signals that upstairs is a comedy club, while downstairs is the bar. A smaller black chalkboard sign sits at the top of the stairs leading to the bar and says, "Trivia Night—know-it-alls welcome, but leave your condescending attitude at the door."

Sassy. Interesting.

I carefully step down the stairs, not wanting to trip in my heels and make the least graceful entrance possible. The moment my feet land on the last step, I glance up and immediately see Trent and his brother, Tristan. Trent's bodyguard sits discreetly behind them, sipping on a water as his gaze watches all the patrons in the room. Trent's cerulean-blue eyes instantly light up the minute he sees me, and it's impossible to stop my lips from spreading into a huge, giddy smile. His face is open and honest, and it's something I didn't realize I'd missed until now. When I get to their table, he stands to greet me, and I give him a quick hug before turning to Tristan.

"Hey, Tris! It's been ages; how the hell are you?" I ask as I lean toward him and give him a hug. Tristan has filled out a lot since the last time I saw him in person.

"I'm good, just doing the band thing."

I let out a small laugh. The band thing makes it sound so small compared to how big they've gotten in the past few years. You're no longer a small band when you've made it on the cover of *Rolling Stone Magazine*.

"Where are Robbie and Jo? I'm surprised they're not here. You guys were always attached at the hip." Robbie and Tristan have been best friends for as long as I can remember. Wherever one went, the other was right there too. I wondered if things would change when Robbie fell head over heels in love with Jolie when they were fifteen, but she never got between them. It didn't surprise me when Robbie married her five years later, although I could never in a million years imagine getting married at only twenty. Hell, I just turned twenty-six and it's only in the last year that I started feeling like I was ready to settle down and get married. Of course, that's when I thought I'd be settling down with Brad.

Ugh, fuck that guy.

"Jolie's got the flu, so they stayed home tonight." Thank God for Tristan, or else who knows where my thoughts would've spiraled to.

"Bummer. Well, maybe another time we can all get together. It'd be great to see everyone from the old neighborhood."

"Kasen and Miles would've come, but Kasen decided to go to

a party in the Hills, and Miles thought he might need a chaperone," Trent explains.

"Since when does Kase need a chaperone?"

Trent and Tristan share a look that tells me there's a lot more going on than they're willing to say. They do that brother thing where they have a complete conversation with just their eyes before Trent turns to me and says, "We can't really talk about it."

"Got it. I'm not quite in the trust circle yet, right?"

Trent looks increasingly uncomfortable and shoots another look to Tristan, who simply responds, "Something like that. We've learned not everyone can be trusted, even when we've known them since we were kids."

I turn a questioning look to Trent. He sighs heavily and rubs his neck. "You remember Jesse, Miles's brother?"

"Yeah, what about him?"

"He sold a story to the tabloids back when we were first starting to take off," Trent says.

"He sold out his own brother?"

"People do a lot of stupid shit for drug money," Tristan says, disdain dripping from every word. His gaze is hard, and his hands are gripping his beer bottle so tightly that his knuckles are starting to turn white. I'm reminded that their mom chose drugs over them, which led to them living with their aunt and uncle—which was probably the best thing for them both since their uncle was a great guy and the one who got them started with music.

"I'm so sorry you guys had to go through that. I get the hesitancy to share. It's no big deal. I don't need to know."

Trent's deep blue eyes shine with a look I can't quite describe—maybe a mix between curiosity, respect, and appreciation. He opens his mouth like he wants to say something but is interrupted by the emcee for tonight's trivia night.

"Welcome, everyone, it's nineties night, which means all the trivia questions are nineties themed. Let's hope you remember the decade that is coming back with a vengeance. So, just a reminder how tonight goes. Each table is a team, but no table can have more than six people. All trivia questions will be displayed on the monitors—there are three, one back at the bar, and then one on each side of the stage—and on the tablets at your table, which is also where you'll input your answers." He points to each of the monitors and uses the table closest to him to point out the tablet that looks like a really thick iPad. "There will be five rounds with five questions each, and we'll update the standings after each round. Any questions?"

When no one says anything, he smiles and says, "Then let the games begin! What 1990s teen movie was retitled after a song by Britney Spears?"

Oh shit, I know this!

I grab the tablet and input *Drive Me Crazy*. I look up at Trent and Tristan who are staring at me with matching bemused expressions. "This game was made for me. I love everything about the nineties. The music, the sitcoms. They don't make 'em like that anymore."

"Lock in those answers!" the emcee shouts as all the monitors start displaying a red pulsing screen and a countdown. When it hits zero, all the answers entered on the tablets pop up. Correct answers are shown in green and incorrect answers in red. Our table and two others got the correct answer. I beam at both the guys, and Trent smiles wide.

"Alright, folks, next question. What was the first animated feature film to be nominated for a Best Picture Oscar?"

Both Trent and Tristan immediately look at me, eagerly awaiting my answer. "Oh, come on, is this whole game going to be on my shoulders?"

"Hey, you're the one who said you love the nineties. We're just letting the queen do her thing," Trent says with a smile that is far sexier than it should be.

Wait, no. Not sexy. I cannot find Trent sexy. He's a rock star. His life is spent touring and being surrounded by gorgeous women. He's not the stable, put-together guy I'm looking for. He may not be an asshole, but he's still not what I need. Besides, I came here tonight determined to firmly reestablish our friendship, not flirt with him.

"Okay, fine. Uh, give me a minute." I'm thrown off. God, I can't believe I thought Trent was sexy. I haven't had the hots for him since we were teens. Now is not the time for this.

I start thinking about the question and all the random, typically useless trivia I have about the nineties in my head. Animated feature in the nineties will most likely be a Disney movie. Despite the fact I work in the film industry now—at least in some capacity—I was never all that invested in the Oscars, so I have no idea.

I shrug my shoulders. "I'm at a loss, guys."

"*Beauty and the Beast*," Tristan says casually.

Trent and I both stare at him, our mouths gaping slightly.

"What?" He shrugs like it's no big deal. "It was Jolie's favorite. She loved the library."

The monitors start blinking red and I quickly type it in. When the results show up, Tristan's answer turns out to be the correct one.

"Wow, that was impressive."

"If it has to do with Jo, Tristan knows all about it," Trent says before taking a sip of his water.

Tristan shoots him a glare but doesn't say anything. Clearly I'm missing something, but I decide not to press. We finish the round, only missing one question out of the five, when the emcee announces there will be a five-minute break.

"I thought you were here to hook Becka up with someone. Seems you're slacking," Tristan says.

Trent's jaw—his very defined jaw with just the slightest hint of stubble—clenches before he looks around the room. He tilts his chin and gives a small nod to a group of guys two tables away from us.

"What do you think of the blond guy? That's Cooper. He's a good guy."

"Blond guys aren't really my type."

"Ah, right. You like them tall, dark, and preppy."

I'd take offense, but that's exactly the type of guy I've dated pretty much my entire life. Trent might be the closest to "bad boy" that I've ever liked and that was so long ago, I doubt it counts. Not to mention, Trent may look like a bad boy, but he's far from it. The more time we spend together, the more I can tell that my initial judgment was correct. He's still a good guy.

"Alright, what about the brunette next to him? That's Scott." Trent turns to Tristan. "Scott's still single, right?"

Tristan nods. "I'm pretty sure."

"He's a good guy. Works for a tech firm and only does serious relationships. I don't think I've ever known the guy to have a one-night stand."

Tristan excuses himself to go get us all another round of waters, and I take the opportunity to be honest with Trent. I fold my hands on the table and lean forward. "Actually, as much as I appreciate you agreeing to be my dating coach, I've been thinking about it the past few days and think it'd be better if I take a break from dating. Give myself a reset and all that."

His body mirrors mine, and it reminds me of when we would sit in the cafeteria together and swap stories about our days across the table. "That's not a bad idea. That's what I've been doing too."

"I, uh, I read about your breakup a few months ago. I'm sorry." My cheeks flush because I totally just gave away the fact that I've been watching his band, or at least news about him.

He shrugs it off. "I should've seen the signs sooner. And I'm not at all surprised that the news blew up the way it did. I'm sure she fueled those flames. She loved the attention."

"How'd you two get together anyway? Liv Warren seems like the complete opposite of you." Liv Warren is an actress who's notoriously high-maintenance.

"It started out as a publicity stunt for her new movie. One of our songs was on the soundtrack, and the studio was looking to hype up some excitement for the film. Her costar was already engaged or else they probably would've considered putting him and her together. Either way, I was single and the timing worked, so I said okay. But I guess I was never that good at acting, and even though she's outrageous in front of the camera, she was more down-to-earth behind closed doors. We spent a lot of time together when we didn't have to and decided to make it real. We dated for a few months before I realized she was just acting."

"You don't think any of it was real."

He leans back against the seat and tilts his head up at the ceiling before looking back at me. "I can't be sure anymore. I look back on our time together, and I can't tell what was real and what was fake. I think that's what pissed me off so much. I'd never doubted myself like that in a relationship, and I didn't like feeling like what I thought was real was just some step up the ladder for her."

He picks at the edge of his beer bottle—the only one he's had all night—his mouth turned down in a frown that makes me want to move to his side of the booth and hug him.

"I'm so sorry you had to go through that, Trent. You didn't deserve to be treated that way."

Once again he shrugs it off. "Just remind me never to date anyone famous again, okay?"

He's talking like I'll be around to advise him on his love life, and I admit it thrills me that we both seem to be needing our friendship again.

"Do you have much free time before you leave for tour? I'll admit I don't know all the prep it takes to get ready for a tour."

"I'll have some. Why?"

"Want to hang out with me? I could really use a good friend these days, and I didn't realize how much I'd missed you."

His lips quirk up in a smile and his blue eyes shine. "I'd love that—more than you could ever know."

5

TRENT

Never in a million years did I think I'd be prepping for an eight-month-long tour to sold out crowds upward of twenty thousand people. I hoped for it. Oh man, did I hope for it. But it was one of those things that seemed too impossible to ever really happen.

And yet, here we are. The details are finalized, and Robbie's buzzing around the room like a ball of energy gearing up to get everything ready. I sometimes imagine that he'd probably be a really successful CEO of some Fortune 500 company if he hadn't gotten swept up in our band stuff. I'll never tell him that though. We couldn't afford to lose him.

"Anyone want anything to eat? I'll make us some lunch," Robbie offers as he heads toward my kitchen while the rest of us stay in the living room. Everyone nods or mumbles, all of us lost in our own thoughts.

Kasen's texting on his phone, probably setting up his next party, but will no doubt be joking with Robbie again soon. I swear those two could be the next Abbott and Costello. If Robbie was ever on the hunt for a new best friend, I'm sure Kasen would be first in line. Miles sits next to him, drumming his hands on his legs to the beat of one of our songs while he talks about the Prince Albert piercing he just got. Personally, I'd rather hear about his kinky sex life than his dick piercing, but maybe that's just me since none of the other guys are saying anything.

Tristan is sitting in the corner, writing in the notebook he uses for lyrics. His gaze darts around the room, occasionally lingering on Jolie where she sits on the couch, her laptop on her lap, editing images of our last band shoot. She'll be our tour photographer and always posts on our social media for us.

My fingers absently strum the guitar in my hands as my mind swirls with how far we've come and all the ways we've changed since those teenaged boys with big dreams. Somehow along the way, I got deemed the responsible one. I suppose I am now, but it wasn't always that way. When the band first started up, I was your stereotypical rock star. It was easy to get sucked into the crazy life—women, alcohol, parties. I never did drugs; after my mom died, I swore I'd never touch them and I haven't. But I lived hard for that first year or two that we were really hitting it big. We all did.

But then Kasen nearly overdosed and that was a huge wake-up call for me, for all of us really. We decided to chill out for a while, and within a few weeks, all our so-called friends completely disappeared. That was when I realized how fake all of it was. People just wanted a piece of us because we were topping the charts. They didn't really care about any of us. I wasn't the only one who noticed the disappearing act, and apart from Kasen, we all agreed to only rely on each other.

That's when I fully embraced my role as caretaker and papa bear of the band.

Since then, I've become the de facto responsible one who keeps the family in line. Miles is the long-haired drummer who is chill and fun and always down to smoke a joint if it's offered. Kasen is the tatted-up party boy who plays as hard as he rocks out on his bass. And Tristan is the stoic playboy while he secretly pines for the woman he can never have.

Sometimes being the papa bear is fucking exhausting. Besides watching over Miles, Kasen, and Tristan, I also work with Robbie on the band management side. He doesn't really need my help, but I like knowing what's going on, and Robbie doesn't mind. He's as dedicated to the band as the rest of us, and I'm endlessly thankful that Tristan brought him into our life.

I glance over at my brother again to see him discreetly watching Jolie who's now in the kitchen wrapping a Band-Aid around Robbie's finger. That guy is the most accident-prone person I've ever met, but he's also one of the happiest and nicest guys in the world. He never has a bad thing to say about anyone and can defuse a bad situation in sixty seconds flat. He's also as loyal as they come and has been like a second brother to me since he and Tris were in kindergarten.

I wish my brother was just watching Robbie as he gets fixed up from slicing his finger with a knife while he was trying to cook something, but I know his gaze is solely focused on the redhead laughing as she stands between Robbie's legs.

I glance at Miles, who's now surfing through the hundreds of channels on my TV, and then lean over and whisper to Tristan, "You need to move on."

He doesn't even bother to deny it. "I will."

He won't. He's been in love with Jolie since the very moment he laid eyes on her. But his best friend got to her first. When he saw how happy she was with Robbie, he stepped back. That's why he's never had a serious relationship, or any relationship that wasn't just sex. That's the reason he's embraced his life as a bachelor playboy even though he's only twenty-four.

I'm pretty sure my baby brother will love her until the day he dies, which breaks my heart because no one knows my brother like I do.

He's got so much love inside of him, even after all the shit we went through as kids. And I know for a fact, if he could just let Jolie go, he'd be able to find someone who he can finally share all of that love with instead of living an unfulfilled life with just one-night stands. That might be the dream for some guys, but I know it's not enough for Tristan. It's just what he settles for.

"I gotta pee," Kasen says, standing up dramatically.

"Thanks for sharing," I reply as he walks away.

Settling on *The Big Lebowski*, Miles sets the remote on my coffee table, glances down the hall toward where Kasen disappeared, and then pierces me with his brown gaze. "I'm worried about Kase."

That catches my attention. "Why? Did something happen?"

He rubs his short beard. "I thought I saw Charli at that party we went to in Malibu the other night."

My blood runs cold. "Charli? I thought she moved to Miami."

Two years ago, Kasen almost overdosed on drugs supplied by Charli, the girl he'd been seeing at the time. She's a party girl who's become famous—or infamous—for supplying the highest quality goods. She's connected to all the best hot spots and hooked Kasen the first time we partied with her back in the day. He thought he loved her, but I knew he didn't. He was too consumed with the drugs, the rush and high she provided him. But that's literally the only thing he knows about her. Charli is a chameleon. She becomes whatever you want her to be. She's anything but real, but Kasen's always been too high to realize that he's enamored with a woman who's put him on a one-way path to destruction. After his almost overdose, he promised us he'd stop seeing her.

Out of everyone in our band family, Kasen is the one I'm the most worried about.

"So did I, but I swore it was her. Her hair's blonde now and she's thinner than I remember, but drugs will do that to you."

"Did Kase see her?"

Miles lifts his hands in a who knows gesture. "I didn't see them together, but if I saw her, he could have."

"And you're sure it was her?"

"Not one hundred percent, but I'm pretty sure."

"Well, I guess it's a good thing we're leaving for tour soon. He can't hang out with her if we aren't here, but I definitely want to keep an eye on him. I don't know that there's anything we can do until we confirm there's a problem. I haven't noticed him acting like he did when he was partying with her before." I look over at my brother. "How's he been with you?"

"His usual self. He hasn't mentioned Charli at all."

"That's what worries me," Miles says. "He knows we don't like her or how she gave him bad shit and then left him in that seedy motel." He looks at me. "I don't think he'll say anything if he's seeing her again. I think we need to just be extra observant and look for the signs. If he's using again, I want to catch him early and get him the help he needs."

Miles takes a puff from his vape pen that he uses to smoke weed—all the high, but none of the smell. I look over to Tristan to see him taking a sip of his beer. He never drinks more than two—neither of us do—but we aren't exactly saints either.

"Maybe we need to have a clean tour."

"What do you mean?" Miles asks.

"I mean no drugs, no alcohol. We all know it's a slippery slope. Maybe Kasen has a few beers and then smokes a little weed, but how long before that's not enough for him anymore and he goes back to pills or cocaine? Or worse? But if we stay clean and sober maybe that'll help him."

"He's still gonna go to parties," Tristan points out.

"Probably. We can't stop him, but we can go with him and keep an eye on him. Look out for him," I say.

Miles rubs his bearded chin. "Weed helps with my anxiety, but I suppose I could try not using it for this tour."

"If it gets too bad, let me know and we'll figure out something else. I was just thinking this could be a way to minimize his temptations," I say.

"It's a good idea. I'm in. Whatever it takes to make sure Kasen stays clean, I'm all for it," Miles says.

Tristan nods in agreement just as the bathroom door swings open and Kasen wanders back out to my living room.

"Let's go practice while Robbie makes lunch. We can talk more tour details later," Kase says, completely unaware of what we were just discussing.

Miles grabs his sticks, Kasen picks up his bass, and Tristan grabs his guitar from his room, since we live here together. We all meet in the studio, which is a room I converted when I bought the house. Before long, we're lost to the music, and as I sing into my microphone, I feel a peace settle over me that only comes when I'm singing. The music wraps around us, and it feels more like home than any physical place ever has.

6

BECKA

The pen scratches across the paper before getting handed off to Trent who's sitting across from me. Simone beams with pride and excitement as she takes the now-signed contract from Trent and tucks it away in her project folder.

"Well, gentlemen, we can't wait to see how it all turns out. There's a lot riding on the success of this documentary, so no pressure."

Robbie stands and reaches his hand out to shake with Simone. "We're excited about this opportunity."

Today was more of a formality with Fletcher, the documentary director and only Robbie and Trent present to represent the band, since the entire band already signed the initial contract. This was an addendum added regarding promotion expectations and finalizing details for filming.

The rest of our team stands from the table and starts to make their exit when Trent's voice catches my attention.

"You got any plans right now?"

I glance at him to make sure he's talking to me, and our eyes lock instantly. "Nope, I was just going to take my lunch break."

His smile grows, lighting up his gorgeous blue eyes. "Perfect.

I'm starving and was going to see if you wanted to grab a bite and catch up some more."

His smile is infectious, and I feel my lips pull up. "Give me two minutes to set my stuff down at my desk. I'll meet you down in the foyer."

"Sounds good."

I exit the room, quickening my pace so I don't keep him waiting when a tall blonde steps in my way, her eyes alight with glee.

"Simone. What's up?"

"Did I just overhear Trent Bridger ask you out on a date?"

Oh, for fuck's sake.

"It's not what you think."

"Bullshit it's not. And while I should be discouraging you from hooking up with someone we're currently working with, I also can't blame you because that man is fine with a capital F."

"I swear, Simone. It's not like that at all. Trent and I are friends. We grew up together in the same small town in Texas. We've known each other too long for me to find him attractive."

That's the biggest lie I've ever told her, but Simone can be like a dog with a bone when she thinks she's got the juicy details on gossip. I need to kill that notion immediately.

She stares me down, searching for the lie. I swear she missed her calling working as an FBI interrogator.

"I don't know whether to be disappointed in you or thrilled that he's still available." She arches her brow, her gaze still staring me down like she hopes I'll crack at any moment and confess my undying love for him.

Not a fucking chance.

Pointing behind her in the direction of my office, I say, "If you don't mind, I need to drop this off so I can get to lunch."

As if just now realizing she's completely blocking my way, she steps aside. "Of course. Don't want you to be late for your lunch with your *friend*," she says with a wink.

Oh good grief. She didn't buy it at all.

Trying to push the interaction aside, I rush to my office, drop all my papers on my desk, grab my purse from my bottom desk drawer, and then hustle to the elevator, praying that I don't run into anyone else.

Trent is waiting for me in the foyer, sunglasses resting in the neck of his T-shirt, a brown leather jacket fitted to his body like he should be on the cover of a men's magazine. Women walk by, their eyes hungry as they drink him in, while he stands there oblivious as he looks down at his phone. The giant looming bodyguard behind him isn't oblivious in the slightest. He gives the women a menacing glare that warns them not to even think about coming within two feet of Trent.

I wonder where his bodyguard was hiding while we were all in our meeting.

Before I have a chance to think any further on the logistics of Trent's life and what it must be like to have someone following him at all times, he glances up, and a heat spreads through my body as his gaze connects with mine and his face lights up with the brightest, most genuine smile I think I've ever seen.

Once again, I find my own smile spreading across my face to match his. "Sorry for taking so long. I ran into Simone in the hall."

"That's okay. I don't mind waiting. I just didn't want to miss an opportunity to catch up some more. Have you tried that Thai place in the Promenade? It looks amazing."

"It is amazing. Best Thai food in Southern California hands down." My mouth waters just thinking about their chicken pad Thai.

Instead of walking the few blocks, Trent ushers me to a Range Rover with black tinted windows. His bodyguard opens the door for us and then sits in the passenger seat next to the driver.

"This is intense. Are you sure you don't want to just order in and eat in my office? They'll deliver it."

He looks at me, confusion filling his handsome features before his gaze shoots to the front seat and then back to me as understanding dawns. "I guess this does seem pretty over the top just to go get lunch a couple of blocks away, but we'd be hounded if we tried to walk there. I figured this was the easiest way to get there without being followed."

"Do you have to do this everywhere you go?"

He shrugs. "Pretty much."

"Wow, I can't imagine living like that."

"Doesn't Will have to deal with this when you guys go out?"

I shake my head. "Not really. Sometimes fans will recognize him and ask him for an autograph, but he's never needed security detail or a fancy driver to go to lunch."

"He's a lucky guy," he says, pursing his lips and looking down at his lap before glancing out the window at the people walking along the sidewalks.

I let the conversation drop because I feel like I just inadvertently touched a nerve. My own gaze looks out my window just as we take a turn.

"Uh, we should've stayed straight. The restaurant is up there on the right."

Trent looks over at me. "They know. We're going in the back to avoid too many people seeing me. With publicity ramped up for the tour, my face is plastered everywhere. Case in point," he says, pointing to a poster displayed in the window of a music store across the street of the band and the dates for their latest tour. "When it gets like this, I usually try to go in the back whenever I eat out just to avoid as much chaos as possible."

I glance back at him just as he looks ahead and see him with new eyes. He looks so much like the Trent I've known for so long, but I can't imagine the burden of having to meticulously plan every action. He's not that simple boy who grew up in a small town in Texas. Not anymore.

We pull up behind the restaurant, and his bodyguard guides us inside. A waitress is ready to direct us to a table tucked away in the back and with a privacy screen that mostly shields us from the other lunch patrons.

We place our order, and I decide to keep the conversation

light, wanting to veer away from anything that might give him that melancholy look he got ever so briefly in the car. The conversation shifts effortlessly between my job, the band and their upcoming tour, Will's career with the LA Wolves, and Will's new dog, Rex, that I'm hopelessly in love with.

By the time lunch ends and we're on our way back to my office, my heart feels light from laughing so much. It's been so long since I was able to talk with someone of the opposite sex without any pressure of a date. We were able to just connect and catch up like two friends who forgot how easy it always was with us. There are no expectations except to listen to the other person. To really hear him and have him hear me in return.

It was the best friendly lunch I've had in a very long time.

He drops me off in front of the building, and I lift my hand in a wave as he drives away, my smile still glued to my face.

By the time I've made it back to my desk, I'm already hoping we can do that again before he leaves for tour.

7

TRENT

The bright light of my eighty-six-inch TV flashes in front of me, while some meaningless infomercial plays on. The inky black of the night sky tells me I should be sleeping, but I'm too hyped up after our meeting at VibeTV today. There's something about seeing Becka again that has my mind on overdrive, rethinking every interaction and the way she smiled. Seeing her eyes light up as we reminisced about old times. That craving in my soul that's been growing for months was sated in her presence, and I'm dying to feel that peace again.

Taking a chance, I grab my cellphone off the dark oak nightstand beside me and quickly compose a text before I can overthink it further.

ME
Hey, you up?

I don't expect a reply since it's so late, so when my phone dings less than a minute later, my heart beats fast and my hands instantly reach for the phone I'd already placed back on its docking station.

> **BECKA**
> Surprisingly yes. Can't sleep. Why are you still up?

> **ME**
> Same reason. Just a lot going on in my head.

I don't tell her a lot of what's going on in my head is about her.

> **BECKA**
> Do you have cable?
>
> What am I asking? Of course you have cable. I bet you've got every channel known to man.

I let out a laugh, a smile already wide on my face and my body relaxing against my pillows as I respond.

> **ME**
> Yeah, I've got satellite TV, why?

> **BECKA**
> Turn to channel 47.

I quickly change the station, following her directions, and find myself on a popular cable station that we used to watch all the time growing up. They're playing *When Harry Met Sally,* and I have to laugh again when I see it's at the diner scene. I'll never forget the first time we saw this playing on this exact channel so many years ago, and Will and I had to awkwardly explain to an eleven-year-old Becka what Meg Ryan was doing. We barely understood it ourselves since neither of us had even had a girlfriend at that point, but we knew enough about sex from things our friends had said and what we'd seen on TV to know what she was doing. Becka, however, was less clued in to those details.

> **BECKA**
> When's the last time you saw this movie?

> ME
> I honestly can't remember.

> BECKA
> Do you remember the first time we watched it together? You and Will thought you were so cool because you knew more than I did.

I stare at my screen, my whole body sparking to life at the idea that we're reliving the same memory, one not at all tied to the life I currently live. The urge to hear her voice becomes too strong, and I quickly click on her contact info. It rings twice before she answers.

"Hey."

"Hey," I say. "I thought this might be easier than texting back and forth."

"Much easier. So, what's keeping you up?"

I hesitate for only a moment, letting out a heavy breath and deciding to give her a partial truth, just leaving her out of it. "I'm always keyed up the closer we get to tour. I trust Robbie implicitly, but there's also a part of me that's a bit of a control freak, so I'm always running through different scenarios in my head and wondering if we've planned for this or that. I think it's just fresher in my mind because of the documentary. That adds a whole different layer to the tour."

"Are you nervous about it? The documentary, I mean?"

"Not really. It's an incredible promotional opportunity, and it's exciting to think people care about us enough to want to see behind the scenes. I guess I'm just not used to my life being filmed 24/7."

Her voice gets softer. "Does it ever exhaust you? Being this huge rock star with fans everywhere you go? Having to take a bodyguard everywhere?"

My sigh this time is filled with all my familiar burdens that I try to shove down, but that have been scraping the surface more often than not lately. "Truth?"

"Always," she says.

"Yeah, it does." We're both silent for a minute, and I can faintly hear the movie playing in the background that matches what's playing on my screen. Clearing my throat, I say, "You know what I was thinking just before we ran into each other last week?"

"What?"

"How much I missed the quiet, simple life we had back in Texas. Back before everyone knew who we were."

"It wasn't always simple," she says.

There's a world of meaning in that sentence. She could mean growing up without her dad, or how my mom overdosed when I was thirteen.

"No, I guess it wasn't, but some days it felt a whole hell of a lot simpler than life now."

"You know, when I was a kid I couldn't wait to be an adult and have the freedom to do whatever I wanted."

"And now that you're an adult, you wish you could go back to being a kid without a care in the world."

She lets out a soft chuckle. "Sometimes, yeah. Is that crazy?"

"Nah, I think that's normal."

She's silent for a few minutes, and I watch the movie, waiting for her to respond but also not feeling the need to fill the silence. There's something companionable and relaxing about just sitting on the phone with her like this. Sharing an experience even if we're not together.

"Trent," she says, her voice low and tentative.

"Yeah?"

"Do you ever think about your mom?"

I sit up in bed, my body tensing without my control as I'm thrown back into a slew of memories that some days I wish I could wipe from my mind altogether.

"Sometimes," I respond, my voice now matching hers. "It's hard to think about her."

"Because of how she died?"

A heavy breath escapes my lungs at the same time that my

chest tightens. "Yeah, that and just a lot of shit that went down before my aunt and uncle stepped in. I don't think they knew how bad it was until CPS got involved. It's not something I like to think about."

"Sorry. I didn't mean to bring it up like this. I just…"

I wait for her to finish her sentence, but when she doesn't I prompt, "Just what?"

"I think about my dad sometimes. Wondering how things would've been different if he'd stayed and why we weren't enough for him." The crack in her voice is the only hint of the emotion buried deep inside.

"Have you ever thought of finding him?"

Her breath filters through the phone, and I suddenly wish we were lying next to each other talking about this, though I know that we'd probably never have this conversation if it wasn't for the protection of night and distance.

"Yeah. I've never really admitted that to anyone. I tried once. I found an address that belonged to him in Arizona, but I didn't have the guts to actually fly out there, so I sent a letter. He never responded to it."

"He's an idiot."

"I guess. I know you don't like to talk or think about her, but do you think you'd be different if she'd lived? If she'd gotten clean and stuck around for you?"

"I don't know."

"There are some nights where I can't stop thinking about how different I would be if he'd stayed. If I'd grown up with my dad around instead of constantly wondering why I wasn't enough."

"You are enough, Becka. You always have been. He's just a stupid fuck who didn't know what a good thing he had when it was right in front of his face."

She's quiet for a while, and I don't fill the lull, instead just letting the movie play while we sit in silence on the phone.

"Thanks, Trent. I've really missed you. More than I realized."

"Same, Becks. More than you know."

A beat goes by before she says, "Do you agree with Harry?"

"Huh?"

"That men and women can't be friends."

I open my mouth to respond, but nothing comes out. My impulse answer is to say yes, I agree, but then what does that mean for me and Becks? I need her friendship. She's become a bright light in my life in only a week, and that's not something I'm willing to lose or even take for granted. Unlike her dad, I know exactly what I have in her friendship. She's more valuable to me than gold. I can't go back to feeling the way I did before I ran into her on the street—lost and so much lonelier than I've ever felt in my entire life.

"I think they can be friends. Sex doesn't always get in the way. You just have to have clear boundaries." I ignore the knot that forms in my stomach as the words leave my mouth.

"I agree," she says, her voice soft and sleepy. She lets out a yawn confirming what I thought.

"I should let you get some rest."

"Okay," she says, another yawn escaping her. "Thanks for the phone call. I didn't realize how much I needed someone to talk to tonight. It was nice."

"Yeah, it was." More than nice. It was a balm to my soul, something she's doing with every interaction.

"Good night," she says

"Night," I respond and then the line goes dead. I drop the phone to my lap and continue watching the rest of the movie. As I watch Harry confess his love for Sally, I can't help wondering if I'll come to regret my stance on just being friends, or if keeping her in the friend zone will give me the exact thing I've been searching for.

8

TRENT

My phone beeps, briefly interrupting the music pumping through my ear buds. I put my dumbbells down and grab it from the band around my arm. Becka's name on the screen causes a surprising reaction in my body—my heart beats a little faster, my breathing increases, and my blood rushes south as I picture her beautiful brown hair with caramel highlights, her bright jade-green eyes, and her radiant smile.

Of course, I immediately open up my messages.

> **BECKA**
> Hey! Rooftop Cinema Club El Segundo is hosting a classic tonight, Back to the Future. None of my girlfriends are free. Wanna go with me?

Fuck yes, I want to go with her. I love *Back to the Future*.

> **ME**
> What time?

> **BECKA**
> Movie starts at 8 pm.

> **ME**
> I'll be there.

Suddenly, the day feels like it's going to drag on forever.

I can't wait for tonight.

Fuck me.

I get out of the town car, and my jaw drops at the vision that is Becka. She's always been beautiful, but she's absolutely stunning tonight. I reel in my reaction to her before she notices me. I'm trying to be her friend, not get in her pants.

Not that I could, given the skintight pants she's wearing tonight that hug every perfect curve and make my mouth water. She's also wearing a fitted sweater that goes up to her neck but still manages to make her breasts look amazing.

Not that I'm looking at her breasts.

I'm not.

Okay, I totally am, but I'm trying not to. Goddamn.

Becka glances up from her phone, and the smile that lights up her entire face when she sees me makes my heart nearly stop.

Friends. We're just friends. I need her as my friend.

My lips curve up in a genuine smile, and I walk toward her, leaning over to give her a brief hug—because a lingering one might send the wrong message—once I reach her. Fuck, she smells amazing. Like she just spent the day at a tropical beach somewhere.

She waves at Chris behind me, who gives her a head nod but doesn't say anything. He's not the most talkative guy in the world.

Her eyes are bright when she looks back at me, and for a moment I have to catch my breath. "Thanks for joining me. I tried to get my girlfriends to come, but they were all busy."

"So what you're telling me is I wasn't your first choice. I'm just the consolation prize."

She looks horrified and grabs my bicep while putting her other hand on her chest. "Oh my God, no. I didn't mean it like that."

Right now I don't care how she meant it; the feel of her hand gripping my arm is doing weird things to my body. "It's all good. It's probably good for my ego to not be someone's first choice."

She scoffs and removes her hand, leaving my arm feeling cold where her hand had been. "Right, because your ego is so huge," she says sarcastically. "I almost forgot you're a famous rock star who's used to getting any woman he wants."

Well, maybe not every woman. There's one in particular who's looking pretty good right about now.

Shit, I really need to pull my thoughts out of the gutter.

She rolls her eyes but lets out a light laugh. "Come on. Let's go grab our seats." She leans down and grabs a beach bag I hadn't even noticed resting at her feet.

"What's all that?"

"Oh, just blankets for when the sun goes all the way down and it gets chilly."

"Smart thinking."

She flashes me another smile and then we make our way up to the rooftop screening area. There are rows of adjustable deck chairs facing a large screen with a three hundred sixty-degree view of Los Angeles. Strings of Edison lights hang around the space to offer some mood lighting, and there's a bar and catering section that even from this distance smells amazing. Another area has a bunch of different games, including giant Jenga blocks. I've never actually been here before, but I love the setup.

We grab some food and drinks and then head to our seats. I notice a handful of people glancing at us and pulling their phones out. No doubt pictures of Becka and me will end up online somewhere. I look back at Chris and he nods, already aware of the people he'll likely be talking to if they continue to take pictures. Apart from that, the only real downside to this place is that they provide personal headphones for every movie-goer, which wouldn't be such a bad thing, but I find it doesn't really allow for Becka and me to talk much or for me to hear her reactions.

While the headphones allow me to be completely immersed in the movie, I find myself glancing over at Becka just to watch how her face lights up at certain scenes. I enjoy seeing the way her lips quirk up at the corners and her eyes get soft during the part where he talks about his girl, or when something funny happens and she laughs, or when her expression gets serious and her lips move as she recites the line from memory.

By the time the movie's over, all I can think about is Becka. Everything feels like it revolves around her—what can I say to make her laugh? What can I do to get her to put her hand back on my arm?

As we quietly make our way back down to the street, I rack my brain for ways to draw out this night with her.

"Do you want to grab a drink or something?"

She smiles up at me, and my heart does that pitter-patter thing it's been doing all night when she looks at me. "Sure. That'd be great."

"I know of a great place just down the street that serves all these old-fashioned mixed drinks. I haven't been there in about a year, but it was great last time I was there."

"Sounds perfect," she says.

We wander down the street and while the silence feels deafening to me, Becka doesn't seem bothered by it in the slightest. I glance back to see Chris behind us, like he's been all night long. I look back over at Becka, but she doesn't seem bothered by his presence.

But for the first time in a long time, I am. I'm bothered that I can't be just a guy here with her, but someone who needs protection. Once again, the longing for normalcy hits me like a punch to the gut, but before it can suck me down into its depths, her hand grazes the back of mine as it sways softly against her side.

"Oh, sorry," she mumbles.

"It's all good," I say softly while I wonder how I can make it happen again.

"So, when did you move to LA?" I ask her, needing to hear her voice to keep my mind from spiraling with thoughts I shouldn't be having. I don't know much about her life since Texas, or even what brought her out here to LA, although I can guess.

"When Will got drafted by the Wolves straight out of college. He's been lucky to play with them so long and not get traded as many others have, but he and Jack Fuller, the quarterback, are such a power duo that the team has worked hard to keep him. I'm grateful for that because now that I've lived here for so long, I'd hate to leave."

"Did you go to UT like Will?" Will graduated from the University of Texas in Austin, but I realize now he never once mentioned if Becka went to school there with him.

"I did. I loved it there, and it was nice to still be able to be close to my family. That's the one downside of living in LA. I'm so far away from my mom and Elise."

"Where did Lainey end up?"

"She's here too, well, sorta. She lives in Laguna Beach, so she's not exactly close, but she's not too far either. About an hour and a half if there's no traffic."

"Do you get to see her often?"

"Yeah, we have a girls' brunch regularly with two of our good friends."

"Do you think you'd ever move back to Texas?"

Her expression turns thoughtful, and she nibbles her bottom lip before finally saying, "You know, I don't think so. At one point I thought I would, just to be close to my mom and Elise again. But LA has become home. I may not always love the culture here because it's very different than Texas and often times feels shallow, but I love all the experiences you can have here. I love the sandy beaches, the sunny days that aren't filled with massive humidity that makes my hair frizz up, hearing the soft crash of the waves as they hit the shore while I'm lying in bed. I'll take all of that if I have to deal with the occasional entitled prima donna. What about you?"

"Move back to Texas?" She nods. "Nah, probably not. The band is here, and I could never move away from them. They're my family. The only people I have left back in Texas are my aunt and uncle, and we try to visit them as much as we can and I call them once a week. But Texas hasn't felt like home for a long time."

We both walk in silence, but it doesn't feel heavy; it feels peaceful. I feel comfortable to just be. And I'm not really sure what to do with that, because even though I keep telling myself I just want her as my friend, my reactions and my feelings are saying something completely different.

9

BECKA

The clattering of silverware and the deep hum of conversations greet me as I enter Plum, my biweekly brunch spot. Every other Sunday, my sister Lainey and our friends Gwen and Beth meet here to eat brunch together and catch up on what's been happening in our lives. Lainey lives in Laguna Beach but never misses a brunch. Gwen and I met when I first moved to LA and we were roommates. I got incredibly lucky. I've heard so many horror stories from other friends about their roommate disasters. Many joked that living in LA was like playing roommate roulette, where you never knew which one would be the best or the worst. Even though we don't live together anymore—Gwen lives with her boyfriend, Patrick, now—we're still close and hang out often. We even attempted to take a spin class together—where we subsequently thought we were going to die—which is where we met Beth.

Yeah, spin classes aren't for us.

Gwen, Beth, and I bonded after that first and only class and now try to hang out as often as possible.

I spot Lainey sitting at a booth near the front window and make my way toward her. She sees me and stands up to give me a hug, squeezing me a little tighter than normal, and I pull back to get a better look at her. She's not wearing as much makeup as she typically does, and her eyes have a slightly hollow look to them with blue circles underneath that her minimal makeup can't hide.

"Hey, sis, everything okay?"

Her eyes water slightly, and she gives me a shaky smile. "Not really."

I gesture to the booth. "Let's sit and you can tell me what's going on."

We take a seat in the booth, and Lainey wipes under her eyes. Her gaze avoids mine, and my stomach sinks. Did something happen with our mom or Elise? No. There's no way. Will would be the first one to know, and he would've told me.

"Paul and I broke up."

My eyes go wide and I sit back in my chair, completely surprised. "Why? What happened? I thought things were going so well with you two."

"They were, or at least I thought they were. I just..." She looks out the window, her eyes not focusing on the beautiful view that drew us to this restaurant to begin with. She turns to me, her gaze both fierce and vulnerable. "Do you ever feel like you're broken? Like there's something wrong with you?"

My heart speeds up because I've had those exact feelings more times than I can count. "Sometimes."

She nods and her eyes start to water, but she purses her lips together and holds them at bay. My sister rarely cries, so I know this is hitting her harder than she's letting on.

"Paul said I kept him at arm's length. He wanted someone who would be completely vulnerable with him. He said I wasn't meeting his needs." She grabs her paper napkin and twists it in her hands, back to avoiding my gaze. "He said I had abandonment issues from Dad leaving us." She scoffs and rolls her eyes, "So clearly he then goes and abandons me."

My lips turn down in a frown as defensiveness fills my voice. "He psychoanalyzed you? What a fucking prick. Just because he's a psychologist doesn't give him a right to treat his girlfriend like a patient."

She nods her head and then finally meets my gaze. "I think he's seeing someone else already. Or maybe he was even before he broke up with me. I can't be sure, but I saw him at the Farmers' Market, and he was holding some other woman's hand."

"Fuck him then. You deserve someone whose ego isn't the size of planet earth."

She goes back to fiddling with her napkin and not looking at me. "Do you think he's right? Do you think I have abandonment issues from Dad?"

I watch my sister carefully, noticing the way her shoulders sag with defeat, which is so unlike the take-charge woman I know her to be.

Picking my words carefully, I say, "I think Dad leaving affected us all in a lot of different ways. Elise doesn't even remember him, but she's still super cautious with men. I think it helps that Mom and Doug have been together for so long now." I think about my own dating disasters and try to look at my reactions from a new perspective. "Maybe Dad's abandonment did kind of mess us up. None of us have had successful relationships, but that doesn't mean we can't learn from our past mistakes and do things differently in the future."

I think about how I tried to do things different with Brad, how different I thought he was, but the more time I spend thinking about him and our relationship, the more I can see the cracks. He was attractive, but looks aren't everything. They eventually fade. But personality and compatibility are what makes a difference. I want someone who makes me laugh, pushes me to try new things, and is always down to do something fun. I want someone who will explore with me, challenge me, and grow with me.

Brad was never that guy.

But I refuse to give up, especially now after this conversation with Lainey. She might be the oldest, but she's also always been someone who watches and sees how things are done before she attempts to try them. Maybe I can show her that real love is possible. That we can meet guys who won't leave us behind like we mean nothing. That we aren't destined to always be abandoned.

Gwen and Beth arrive together before Lainey and I have a chance to continue our conversation. As they walk to our table, laughing at something, Lainey gives me a look that begs me not to say anything about Paul. She hates being the center of attention or having people fuss over her, and she needs time to process things.

I get it. I give her a brief nod, and her lips tilt up in a small, grateful smile.

More than ever, I want to prove to my sister that we Edmonson girls are not as broken as our past shitty relationships suggest. That we're worthy of being loved.

That someday we'll find men who will fight for us instead of breaking our hearts.

10

Becka

I look at the address on my phone and then back at the insanely large mansion in front of me. Is this the right place? I'm about to call Trent when I see him open the massive front door and walk out to greet me.

"Thanks for agreeing to join me. I know it was last minute," Trent says as I get out of my car.

"You promised me a beach bonfire. I'll never turn that down."

When Trent texted me last night asking if I was free today to hang out with him at the beach, I didn't hesitate to say yes. I know his time in town is limited, and it's been really nice reconnecting with him. We agreed to meet up after I got off work. I had recommended one of the public beaches, but he said there'd be too great a chance that he'd be recognized and we'd have a flock of paparazzi and fans hounding us. Instead he suggested his friend's place in Malibu since he has beach access and a firepit on the back patio.

I'm a sucker for a firepit, especially one at the beach.

I'll never forget when Lainey and I first moved to California after Will got drafted to the Wolves. We both wanted a change from life back in Texas. Lainey got a job in Laguna Beach and I got my job at VibeTV in Santa Monica so we couldn't live together, but we made a promise to have a weekly sister beach date. We imagined beautiful sandy beaches, hot lifeguards, sexy surfers, and drinking and laughing around bonfires with other LA transplants. We quickly discovered that there's actually only a handful of beaches that you can legally have a bonfire on. And they usually get busy early.

So, this seems perfect to me. There's no way I could've gotten off work and driven to a public beach and still been able to nab a firepit. Not a chance.

I grab my oversized beach bag from my backseat and then follow Trent through the house that looks like a Thai-inspired oasis. There are teak floors, lush gardens on the property, and it has a very vacation vibe to it.

Trent points out several of the bathrooms as we make our way through the house and informs me that there are a total of fourteen bathrooms here.

What does anyone need with fourteen bathrooms? Hell, having two sometimes feels like a huge luxury. I can't even fathom needing fourteen.

We walk through the house, and I fight hard to maintain my cool.

I live comfortably, especially by LA standards, but this is way beyond my norm or even what any of my friends are used to. Hell, even Will's famous football friends don't live in houses as big as this, at least not the few I've been to. It's taking everything in me not to fawn over how stunning and gorgeous every detail of this house is, especially when I realize that Trent doesn't seem all that fazed.

But then, why would he? This *is* the norm for him.

When Trent pushes open the double doors that lead outside, I can no longer maintain my composure.

"Holy. Fucking. Shit."

Okay, well maybe I could've tried to be a little more composed than that. But for fuck's sake, this place is insane.

Trent just laughs. "I told you it would be worth it."

I shake my head in disbelief. "This is beyond worth it. This is breathtaking. Your friend gets to wake up to this view every day?"

"Uh, no. He only lives here a few months out of the year. He splits his time between several different residences."

I turn to him, my jaw practically on the floor and my mind unable to process this. *Does not compute* is repeating in my head. How could anyone not want to live here year-round? Or at least all during the summer when it's sunny and warm, but you've got the cool breeze coming off the Pacific to keep you cool.

"I...I don't even know what to say. I can't imagine having so many houses that you only stay in them for a couple of months a year."

"Yeah, well, Spencer's not great about setting down roots, and he has more money than he could ever spend in ten lifetimes, so he likes to throw it around. He lets me hang out here whenever I'm in town since he's rarely here."

"That's so wild to me. You have friends who live completely different lives than the rest of us."

The realization hits me like a ton of bricks. You'd think the bodyguard would've done it, but no, it's this moment that truly cements for me how famous he is. Trent is way out of my league. I gaze at him with new eyes, seeing him for the rock star he is. His short chocolate-brown hair, his ocean-blue eyes, his rugged good looks and perfect jawline with just the right amount of stubble to look sexy instead of homeless. The tattoos that peek from beneath his shirt sleeves and spread down one of his arms. Why didn't I realize before that he's so different from the boy I once knew? Well, kind of knew since we stopped spending much time together after that kiss freshman year. After that, he became more Will's friend instead of our shared one.

But still. Why didn't I notice how much he's changed?

"Stop looking at me like that," he says, his voice serious and more guarded than I've ever heard from him.

"Like what?"

"Like I'm famous." His gaze drops, and he looks vulnerable and sad. "I can't stand that from you." His gaze settles on mine, and the pleading look in his eyes nearly guts me. "Not you, Becks. Please. I'm the same guy you've always known, just a little older and a little more world-weary."

I look again at his arms and his body, noticing how much he's filled out instead of the lanky teen I remember. "I don't remember you filling out a shirt quite like that or having all those tattoos."

His lips quirk up with a hint of a smile. "Okay, so I got some ink and hit the gym, but deep down, I promise I'm still the guy I always was. Please don't look at me different just because I have rich friends."

"I don't want to, but look around, Trent. This is not the world we grew up in. My mom worked three jobs. Your aunt and uncle worked incredibly hard too. We grew up in a small blue-collar town in Texas, which is a far cry from a mansion in Malibu with beach access no less."

He steps forward, taking my hands in his. It's impossible not to feel the zing of electricity that shoots through my body at his touch and proximity.

"Please, Becks. I'll get down on my knees and beg if I have to, but please don't look at me like everyone else does. I need you to look at me like you did when we ran into each other in the middle of a street in Santa Monica, and trivia night, and movie night. I promise you, deep down I'm still that guy you knew back in Texas. The one who threw mud at you when we were kids, who cheered for Will with you at Friday night football games, who held your hair back when you had too much to drink at Sally Ann Lincoln's seventeenth birthday party."

"That's not fair! I had no idea that drink had alcohol in it. All I knew was it tasted fruity and delicious and you know it," I say, pulling one hand from his and poking his chest. I can't believe he remembers that. We weren't even all that close by then, but he still was there for me, even when my date had ditched me.

He smiles, and it's a smile I'm all too familiar with. It's not the smile I've seen on posters or magazine covers. It's not the smile he tosses out when we've been together in public.

This is his Texas smile. The smile he'd always give me when I did something to make him laugh, or when we'd all hang out as a group and do something our guardians would've had our hides for, like the time we "borrowed" Trent's uncle's car and drove it to Dallas for a Foo Fighters concert.

This is the smile of the boy I've known for damn near my entire life.

His eyes soften as he gazes down on me from his six-inch-height advantage. "Thank you," he says softly and gives my hand a squeeze. But he doesn't let go, and I don't ask him to.

Instead we stand there for longer than we probably should, staring at each other. But it doesn't feel weird or awkward.

It feels like coming home.

11

TRENT

I swallow down the lump in my throat as I stare into Becka's chocolate-brown eyes, her soft hands smooth against the calluses of my fingertips from years of playing guitar.

Without a word, I keep her hand in mine and guide her toward where the firepit is already blazing. My heart starts to slow the longer I feel her hand gripping mine, knowing she's still here with me.

Me. Not the persona I wear for the rest of the world, but just me.

My heart nearly seized in my chest when she started looking at me the way everyone else does. Like I'm something greater than I am.

I'm just a man, desperate to be seen for who I *really* am.

And for the first time in years, I'm in the presence of a woman who's done nothing but that from the moment we reconnected. I can't lose the feeling of finally being seen now. It's like turning on the light when you've been trapped in the dark for too long. It illuminates your whole world and makes you realize what you were missing all this time.

I gesture for her to take a seat and then move over to the built-in bar and grab us both a drink. Before I head back to her, I press the button under the bar that connects to the patio's stereo system, and soft music begins to play. It's an alternative mix that I put together over the past few days, my head lost in nostalgic memories of when Becka and I were younger.

A smile curves the corners of her lips, and her eyes light up when she hears the chords of a familiar Nirvana song that I'm pretty sure I played on repeat when we were in middle school.

"It's really no surprise you became a musician. I should've expected it after your obsession with music growing up," she says.

I shrug. I'm not going to deny it. "Music is the most powerful force in the world. It can make you feel sad, happy, hopeful, heartbroken. Who wouldn't be obsessed with something like that?"

She watches me thoughtfully as I walk back over to her and hand her the drink. "Thanks," she says, quickly taking a sip before diverting her gaze to the blazing fire in front of us. I sit beside her as the fire crackles, spitting sparks into the air while Becka stares blankly at the flames, clearly lost in thought.

I'm lost in her. The way the shadows accentuate certain features on her face. The way the light makes her eyes sparkle. The soft curve of her lips and the slow glide of her tongue across them after she takes a drink of her water.

My body is heating in a dangerous way—a way I choose to ignore, reminding myself that I need her as my friend.

A silence settles between us and—just like that night we talked on the phone—it's not an awkward silence, but a comfortable one.

The crashing of the waves against the sand and the crackling of the logs in the fire are the only sounds until she asks, "Is that your guitar?"

I glance at her and see her gaze focused on something to my right. When I look over, my guitar case sits tucked behind one of the spare chairs.

"Yeah. It's a habit to bring it with me wherever I go. I may be the lead singer now, but nothing soothes me quite like playing my guitar."

"Will you play for me?" she asks, her voice not quite timid but also not as confident as I'm used to hearing from her.

"What do you want me to play?"

She shrugs. "Anything you want."

Getting up, I grab my guitar case and then lovingly pull my instrument from the soft red lining. When I sit back down, the guitar rests comfortably on my knees as my fingers glide over the strings, pulling the pick from the place at the top of the neck where I keep it tucked under the strings. With the pick clasped between my thumb and pointer finger, I strum a couple of chords, the sound vibrating throughout my whole body and calming me in a way that nothing else ever has.

Well, almost nothing.

Becka's coming damn close.

"You know, when my uncle gave me this guitar, I looked at him like he was crazy. I wasn't very good at school. I'd gotten in a few fights, mostly because it was the only way to deal with all the feelings I couldn't name from all the shit with my mom. I didn't think I could be good at anything but taking care of my brother. I'd gotten really good at keeping Tris alive, even when it meant stealing money from my mom's purse before she could spend it all on her drug of the week. I always made sure he was fed, warm, and safe—or at least as safe as I could make him.

"I don't know if my uncle realizes that he saved my life the day he placed this guitar in my hands. He gave me something that I'd never had before—an outlet, a drive, a way to work through whatever I needed to without getting anyone else involved. He gave me something I could be good at if I practiced enough. He changed the entire trajectory of my life, and I don't really know how I can ever repay him for that."

Becka's soft hand lands on my arm, pulling my blurry focus from the instrument in my hands to the woman next to me.

I didn't even realize tears had formed in the corners of my eyes, and I easily brush them away before they're able to spill down my cheeks.

"Your uncle is proud of you, Trent. Anyone with eyes who knows your family can see that. He was proud of you in high school well before you ever got famous, and I can only imagine how proud he is of the man you've become."

Doubt snakes through my gut. "I don't know about that. I wasn't exactly a saint when we first started hitting it big."

"Maybe not, but it's part of what's made you the man you are now. It's not always about the choices we've made in the past that define us, but how we let them shape the person we turn into. For what it's worth, I'm proud to know you and call you my friend."

My gaze connects with hers. "It's worth a lot." More than I could ever tell her. Her friendship is saving me in a way I didn't even know I needed.

12

TRENT

The bar is crowded with people eager and excited for us to perform. We try to do a few small local shows whenever we can, and tonight happens to be our last one before the tour starts in a couple of weeks. I peek out from the curtain, but the lights are bright and it makes it hard to see too far into the crowd. I invited Becka to the show and told her she should come hang out backstage with us, but she's still not here and I'm feeling something I haven't felt in a long time.

Nerves.

Not the small hit of nerves I get before every show, but a full-on gut punch which makes me feel like I'm going to puke. I already know she likes our music, but it's different performing in front of someone you know and respect. I want to impress her.

"She still not here?" Tristan's voice calls from behind me. I hear Kasen laugh and Miles let out a little chuckle but I don't turn around.

Fuck those guys.

They've been teasing me mercilessly about Becka, even though I've told them we're just friends. But they don't believe me.

Maybe they shouldn't.

We had a moment the other night at the beach house. I can't

describe what happened, but it felt different than what I'm used to. It felt real.

Which is why I need her to be my friend—and only my friend. The only real I get anymore is from the guys. If Becka and I dated and things didn't work out, I'd lose her completely. She never stays friends with exes—she's been that way since her first boyfriend. No matter how good a friend she might've been with a guy before they dated, once they broke up, he might as well have been dead to her.

I don't think I could stand to lose her, not now. Not when I need her warmth and realness more than I think I've ever needed anything. She's made me feel a kind of contentment I didn't think I'd ever feel. All those nights feeling lost and alone in a sea of people fade into the background whenever I'm around Becka and see her smile, or hear her laugh, or the way she gets really serious and animated when she's talking about something she's passionate about.

She's real, and genuine, and pure. And I can't lose her.

So what if I want her to be impressed with me? That's a totally normal feeling. I'm supposed to want to impress my friends with how kick-ass I am.

I feel Tristan, Kasen, and Miles move to my back and then see their heads pop around me to peek out of the curtain.

"What's she look like now? It's been fucking forever since I've seen her," Kasen says.

"Same soft-looking chocolate-brown hair, but now she's got some lighter highlights." I throw Tristan a look at his description of her. He gives me a *what* shrug and I try not to scowl, but I know I fail miserably when he arches a brow and gets a cocky smirk on his face. I'm definitely not fooling him.

"What are y'all looking at?" a soft, feminine voice says from behind us.

We all whip around to see Becka standing there in black skinny jeans, black ankle boots, and a white shirt covered by a black leather jacket with her brown hair cascading around her shoulders. Her brow is arched, but her pink lips twitch in amusement.

"Just waiting on you, so our good man here didn't lose his shit thinking you'd ditched him," Kasen says as he walks up to her with his typical swagger and lifts her up into a hug. Kasen is six feet four and covered in tats and piercings, but his smile never fails to make him look like he's as innocent as a kitten.

Even if he's not.

"That's not what would've happened," I say with my scowl directed toward Kasen. Miles just chuckles again, and Tristan remains quietly supportive at my side.

Becka giggles as Kasen swings her around and then sets her back down on her feet.

About damn time.

"Hey, Kase. Long time, no see," Becka says as Miles walks up to her, and she gives him a warm smile. "Miles. It's been way too long. How are you?"

"Been good. Living the life. You know how it goes."

"Oh sure. Yep. I totally know what it's like staying in five-star hotels and rocking out in front of thousands of fans. Definitely know all about that." She gives him a teasing wink and then turns to Tristan and gives him a hug. "Good to see you again."

"You too."

Then it's my turn. A surge of giddiness travels through me when she turns her beautiful gaze to me.

Okay, giddiness and those damn nerves.

I can't remember the last time I was nervous around a woman. It's a novel feeling but one I don't mind. Even if I know nothing can ever happen.

"Hey, Becks." Using her childhood nickname helps me focus on the fact that we're just friends.

But it doesn't go unnoticed that the smile she gives me is a little warmer and softer than what she gave the rest of the band.

It's just for me.

"Hey. Thanks for inviting me tonight."

"Did you find parking okay?"

"Yup. Your directions were perfect."

"Good."

"Yeah."

We stand there, staring awkwardly at each other, and suddenly I have no idea how to continue the conversation. I didn't have this problem the other night at the beach house, or any other night we've talked.

Why don't I have any game with this woman?

Because I can't sleep with her. She's just a friend.

Scratching the back of my neck, I point to a couch in the corner that we use for friends and family to watch the show from backstage if they want to. "Uh, you want to sit here for the show? Or we've got some seats reserved out front."

"I'll probably have a better view from out front, right?"

"Yeah."

She smiles, a slow and sweet smile that makes my gut clench with want. "Okay, then show me the way, Mr. Rock Star."

I quickly point out her spot and get Stu, one of the backstage guys, to walk her to the seat since I can't go out there or I'll be swarmed.

I don't watch from behind the curtain to make sure she gets to her seat safely. I also don't watch her hips sway as she walks away, and I definitely don't groan when she licks her lips and laughs at something Stu says when she gets to her seat.

Nope. I don't do any of that at all.

Okay, so I do all of it. But I'm not acting on anything, so I haven't harmed our just friends status.

The show goes off without a hitch. The audience energy is at an all-time high, and we laugh more than we have at our past couple of shows almost entirely due to the great audience. By the time the show ends, I'm drenched in sweat but feeling high on life.

I've never done drugs, but this is always what I imagine the high feels like. Sometimes, I can even understand why my mom chose it over us. It's fucking addicting.

But then Becka walks backstage, her smile bright enough to light our entire show, and I realize I can't understand my mom at all. Because this high? It's nothing compared to what Becka makes me feel.

Adding the two together? It's fucking dangerous. It makes me want things I know I shouldn't. It makes me want to say, "fuck it" and kiss her hard, making up for our horribly sloppy first kiss when we were fifteen.

"You guys! That was amazing! I have goosebumps from how good you were." Becka holds her arm out and sure enough, little goosebumps sprinkle her skin. Kasen wraps his arm around her neck and pulls her head against his soaked shirt, and I have to laugh at the disgusted face she makes, even if it pisses me off that he touches her so freely.

I told them she was off-limits. Kasen needs to cut that shit out.

"Kase, you fucking stink." She pushes out of his hold, and he throws his head back in a boisterous laugh.

"Part of the gig. No one said it was glamorous. This is the sign of a hard night's work. Now it's time to let loose and celebrate."

Miles and I exchange a look, both of us still worried about Kasen and whether or not he's using drugs again.

"Well, don't let me keep you from your shower, because you definitely need it," Becka says, her voice light and teasing, even if her nose is still wrinkled and her lips slightly pursed to suggest she's not entirely joking.

"Give me ten minutes and then I want to show you something," I tell her, nerves swirling in my belly because I've never told anyone besides the band about my post-show tradition.

"Okay. I'll wait here with Robbie and Jo."

"So, where are we going?"

"It's just around the corner."

I look over in time to see Becka look out the window at the residential neighborhood, her expression curious. Hopefully she doesn't think I'm lame that I don't go straight to an after-party after each show. After two more blocks, I turn right and stop in front of a local park.

Becka turns to me, a question in her eyes.

"Like the other guys, my body is always buzzing with adrenaline after a show. Tristan blows off steam by finding a random hookup. Kasen parties, and Miles usually smokes some weed and hangs out with whoever's available or goes home and watches a comedy special. I do this."

"Come to a park at night like a creeper?" she asks hesitantly.

I can't help but laugh at that. It does seem a little weird. "Come on, I'll show you." We get out of the car, and I grab her hand as we walk toward the playground. I don't even think about the action, but it feels right the minute her hand is enfolded in mine.

"No one's ever around after our shows since it's so late. I have the whole place to myself," I explain to her. "There's always a park in every city we go to, so it's something I can do anywhere we go. But it has to have one specific trait."

"What's that?"

"A swing set," I say with a huge grin and pull her directly to two swings.

We sit down, and I immediately push off and kick my legs back working on building up my momentum until I'm going higher and higher, matching the adrenaline still thrumming steadily through me. Becka swings gently next to me, her eyes watching me intently.

"I swing as high as I can go and then…" Using the momentum I've built up, I swing high and jump off when I reach the highest point. My feet land with a thud against the bark mulch, and I throw my hands up in the air like I'm some kind of Olympic gymnast who just stuck his landing. I turn around to face Becka, my heart in my throat expecting her to laugh at me, even as the adrenaline from the show still simmers in my system.

Becka's green eyes are soft as she stares at me. Something shifts in her gaze, and suddenly the air between us feels charged. Then she smiles, and I release the breath I hadn't even realized I was holding.

She isn't laughing at me. She's looking at me thoughtfully, but her smile holds no judgment.

"When did you start doing this?"

I shrug and walk back to my swing, catching it and sitting down, joining her in a soft sway as we talk. "It was after high school, but I can't pinpoint the first time I did it. It's been too many years. Before I started doing this, I would feel really restless after a show—like I had all this energy and no idea what to do with it."

"Seems like it'd be very rock and roll to do drugs and have sex."

"Probably, but I've never done drugs and..." Fuck, I don't want to admit this to her, but I also don't want to lie to her or hold anything back. Rubbing my shoulder and fighting my embarrassment, I confess, "I might've done the sex thing when we first started getting attention. I got wrapped up in everything, and it took me a while to get my head straight. Fame kind of fucks with you. Suddenly you have all these people who give you attention and want to be around you, hear what you have to say. It's not until something serious happens that you realize how fake it all is. I'm not proud it took Kasen's downward spiral for all of us to realize that no one actually cared about us—not really. They cared about what we could do for them."

"That's sad," she says softly.

I nod. It is sad, but it's the truth. Rock stars are only as valuable as their next big hit.

I lean my head on the chain holding the swing and look at her.

It's dark, but there are enough streetlights nearby to show her face clearly.

"I've never told anyone outside the band about this," I confess. She looks at me, and I gesture to the playground. "You're the first. I know people would think it's silly and childish, but that's kinda the point. My mom never took us to the park growing up. She was always too high. And since Tristan is two years younger, I always felt like I needed to look out for him, so I never felt like I got to be a kid. But this…" I glance around, taking in the park and the swings before my gaze lands on her. "This is my chance to be silly and act like a little kid with no one around to judge me."

"Have the guys ever come with you?"

I shake my head, my eyes never leaving hers.

"So, just me then?"

My voice gets soft and low and catches in my throat before I can finally say the words, afraid that maybe our friendship isn't advanced enough for me to be this vulnerable with her. "Just you."

She reaches her hand out, and I immediately take it in my own. She squeezes it gently, her hand soft against mine. "So, should we see who can swing the highest?"

A grin stretches my cheeks, and my heart soars. "You're on."

13

Becka

My feet barely make a sound as I cross the grass toward Will and see Rex, his rescue pit bull, pumping his legs at a frantic pace to chase after a stick Will just threw.

"That is one spoiled dog," I say.

My brother turns and smiles at me. "Hey, Becks, what are you doing here?"

"Oh, you know. Just thought I'd take a stroll."

"Really?" he asks doubtfully.

"No, not really. I was driving to your house and noticed you when I passed by the park."

He laughs. "Yeah, that makes more sense."

We stand together quietly while Will continues to throw the stick every time Rex brings it back. Finally, I break the silence.

"I'm worried about you, Will." He's not been the same since his fiancée died in a car accident a few years ago.

I'll be honest, I hated Candace. I thought she was using my brother, and he let her have too much say over his life. It caused a huge rift between us—the biggest one we've ever had, which made me hate her even more. But regardless of my feelings, her death broke something in Will, and he's never been the same.

He turns to me. "Nothin' to worry about, Becks."

I look at him, my brows pinched with concern. "Lie to yourself all you want, but don't lie to me."

He glances at me, then back out at the grassy field, his jaw clenched tight with anger, but then another look passes across his face, a mix of maybe guilt and devastation. Is he thinking about Candace again? Why can't he see how horrible she was? That he deserves so much more? That he deserves to be happy?

"The look on your face is why I'm so worried about you," I admit. Maybe if I point it out, he'll finally see it too.

He turns to me again, and I watch as he gazes at my crossed arms. I'm prepared to fight him on this. He needs to see what a poison she was to his life. She's hurt him enough. Even in her death, she's still hurting him, and I'm sick of seeing my brother suffer.

"I'm not ready, okay? I get why you're worried, but I can't go there."

"It's been two years, Will. Why are you holding on so tightly to someone who never deserved you in the first place?"

He shrugs his shoulders at my question, which just makes me all the more frustrated.

"That's not an answer. If you won't tell me, then maybe you should see a professional. Either way, you have to talk about this. I can tell it's eating you alive." I reach out and grab his arm, squeezing it in a sign of support. "You don't deserve that, Will."

His expression tells me he doesn't believe me.

"You deserve to fall in love with a woman who can truly love you. A woman who makes your heart soar and makes you feel like you can't function without her."

He scoffs, but his eyes get sad. "I think you've been reading too many romance novels again. That's not real life." He turns back to Rex, not willing to look at me anymore.

"You know what's really sad? It is real life, Will. Yes, people every day settle for so much less than they deserve. They settle for love that feels safe, but there's a difference between safety because you're not risking your heart and safety because you know your heart is being held with care by the one you love. Too many people settle for the former when they should hold out for the latter."

I don't think about the words until after I've said them, but suddenly they slam into me like a brick house, the truth of them forcing me to look at my own recent situation with fresh eyes. I was settling for Brad because I knew what to expect with him—or at least, I thought I did. But if I'm honest, he never made me feel close to what I've felt hanging out with Trent these past couple of weeks. He never made me feel safe, whereas Trent has always made me feel safe and protected. But more than that, he makes me feel alive. Every time we're together, it feels like my veins are fizzing with an energy that's never been there before.

Holy shit.

Am I falling in love with Trent?

"When did you get so wise about love?" Will asks.

"When I experienced the difference," I say a little breathlessly, my mind reeling with my recent realization.

That gets his attention. "What? I didn't know you were seeing anyone."

"I'm not," I say sadly, because Trent and I are just friends. I could mention that I've been hanging out with him. I'm sure Will would love to see him. I know they still talk occasionally, but I don't want to. This is the first time I've felt like I have Trent to myself. I don't want to share him with my brother just yet. Especially if I only get to have him as my friend.

"Did someone break your heart? Whose ass do I need to kick?" Oh jeez. Will's got his overprotective brother face on.

I smile at him, but I can tell that it probably doesn't reach my eyes, especially with how Will looks at me. "I'm a big girl, Will. I don't need my brother to fight my battles." This realization has made me reevaluate things with Trent though. I don't know if I'll be content with just being his friend. "I'm handling it." I say, deciding it's the truth. "But it's made me think about you and your situation. It kills me seeing you torture yourself over

Candace. She doesn't deserve that loyalty, especially when she wasn't even loyal to you."

"Becks, stop, please. I'm just not ready yet."

"I'm worried if you wait until you're ready, you might miss out on the real thing."

He looks worried too, but he gives me that pleading look, and I know he needs me to drop it.

Fine. I'll drop it for now, but only because my own head is spinning.

And because now I'm worried that if I wait, I might miss out on the real thing that's been right in front of me.

14

Becka

I pace along the hardwood floors of my condo, my phone clutched in my hand. My mind is racing almost as fast as my heart.

Am I about to mess things up?

Or am I about to make the best decision of my life?

I talked to Will about safety when risking your heart, but the more I thought about it the more I realized there's risk either way. The safety comes in trusting the other person. In knowing them enough to know your trust in them is worth it. That they'll take this gift you're giving them and treat it like a precious blessing. But to give that gift—your heart—in the first place, you have to risk. Risk your heart. Risk the familiar, the comfortable.

I'm about to risk it all, and I'm panicking.

I texted Trent an hour ago to see if he could come over, and he should be here any minute. I have no idea what to expect. I know there's been something charged between us that's been there from the beginning and has grown with every hangout. But does he feel it too?

If he doesn't, this could be absolutely disastrous, both personally and professionally. I mean, I'm about to be working on his band's documentary, which is big for both of us. If this doesn't go how I hope it does, then that would make work incredibly awkward when he comes back from tour.

I'm either about to make the biggest fool of myself or have the best sex of my life.

My vote's on the best sex.

There's a knock at the door, and my heart catches in my throat. Okay, he's here.

Time to jump.

No risk, no reward, right?

I walk briskly to the door and open it, and my breath stalls in my chest. God, has he always been this sexy? I mean, he's always been hot, but suddenly it's like my libido is on steroids and I want nothing more than to jump on him.

One step at a time.

"Hey, thanks for coming."

His brow furrows in concern. "Sure. You made it seem kinda urgent. Everything okay?"

"Uh, yeah. I was just hoping I could talk to you about something."

"Okay," he says, looking at me with all this trust in his eyes that I start to second-guess myself. What am I doing? He's expressed more than once what my friendship means to him.

Shit. I can't do this.

My shoulders drop and my heart aches, but I try to push it aside. This isn't the first time I've been disappointed, and it likely won't be the last.

"Want something to drink?"

"I'll take a water."

"Go ahead and have a seat. I'll be right back." I watch him head to the couch, briefly admiring how his jeans hug his delicious ass, and then scamper into the kitchen and grab two glasses. I fill them with water, close my eyes, take a deep centering breath, and then head out to the living room.

Instead of sitting, Trent is admiring my view. "This is a great place."

I smile. "Yeah, I fell in love with it instantly. It was a steal considering the view I have."

He turns, and his smile is so magnetic, it draws me to him. I stand closer than is probably appropriate and hand him his water. My heart is racing, even if my mind has already decided I can't pursue anything with him. We're friends, and that means so much to him. Hell, it means so much to me too. Clearly I wasn't thinking when I texted him earlier.

We drink our waters and stare out at the ocean a distance away. There are a couple of smaller condos and a major road that are also in the view, but now that it's night, all you see are the glittering lights, and it looks a little magical.

"So you said you had something to talk to me about?"

Oh shit.

"Uh, yeah, you know what, it was stupid. I figured it out."

His brow arches, and his blue eyes pierce me. My heartbeat speeds up, and I take a sip of my water, hoping he doesn't notice the way my hands are shaking as I place my water glass on a nearby table.

"Are you okay?"

I look up at him and realize he's moved a little closer, his own water glass sitting on the windowsill and our bodies practically touching. God, is he trying to torture me?

"I'm fine," I say, although it comes out as a cracked whisper, and the words sound false even to my ears.

His gaze traces the lines of my face and my blood heats, my body tingling with desire so fierce it makes my knees weak. My gaze is locked on his as I watch his eyes move across my face. I wonder what he sees. Does he see the girl I was back in Texas? The girl he kissed once upon a time? Does he wish that kiss had ended differently? That we had kept going instead of stopping and laughing it off and then never talking about it again?

Does he want to kiss me now as desperately as I want to kiss him?

His hand comes up and brushes a lock of my brown hair

behind my ear, his fingertips grazing the skin, and my eyes close at the pleasure that floods my body at his simple touch.

Maybe it's because my eyes are closed and my other senses heightened, but I swear his breathing gets heavier.

"Becka," his voice is whisper-soft and his minty breath fans my face. I open my eyes to see him leaning down, hunger in his eyes.

Hunger for me.

That's all I need to see. I throw my arms around his neck and pull him down until our lips brush. He lets out a deep groan before his arms wrap around my waist, and he hauls me against him until our bodies are flush. What started as a quick brush of lips turns into the filthiest French kiss I've ever had. His tongue dances with mine, and my hips grind against him of their own accord.

We both groan as the kiss deepens further. Fuck, his mouth is amazing. He definitely didn't kiss this well at fifteen. I quickly get lost in the brush of his mouth against mine, our tongues licking into each other's mouths. Our kiss is greedy and needy and filled with longing.

His need matches mine, and I'm so relieved I could cry. Just friends isn't enough for him either.

Thank God.

But I need more. I push off his jacket and scrape my nails down his arms. He growls, and his blue eyes heat with a blazing lust that leaves me completely breathless. He bends down and throws me over his shoulder, causing a squeal to break free.

"Bedroom. Now."

Fuck me, that's hot.

"Down the hall." Wow, my voice is breathy. But I'm in such a daze of lust I don't even care. I just want to get this man naked and inside me as fast as possible.

He walks down the hall with a speedy gait and no hint of struggle, as if I weigh nothing. He quickly finds my room and drops me on the bed with a small bounce. I'm so turned on, I'm pretty sure my panties are destroyed from how wet they are.

I've never had anyone manhandle me before, and holy shit. It. Is. Hot!

His gaze locks on mine, and everything I'm feeling is mirrored there. We're on the same page.

God, this risk is already so worth it.

He reaches behind his neck and rips his shirt off his body leaving him bare-chested. Why is it so hot when men take their shirts off like that? But then I'm distracted by his ridiculously sexy six pack and golden tan skin. Yeah, Trent is definitely not the lanky boy I grew up with anymore. And I am one hundred percent okay with that. Good Lord.

He starts to undo his belt buckle and then nods at me. "You're a little overdressed, don't you think?"

My eyes widen, and a smile breaks across my face. "Sorry. I was distracted by the view."

He smirks, but then as soon as I take off my shirt, his stare turns hungry again as his gaze caresses every inch of exposed skin. I reach behind my back and unhook my bra. I slide the straps off my shoulder and then let it fall to my elbows before sliding it the rest of the way off and throwing it somewhere in the room—I can't be bothered to care where it lands. I stand up and slide my shorts off at the same time that Trent slides his jeans and boxer briefs down.

My mouth waters at the sight of his dick.

I'm not a nun, okay? I've seen my fair share of dicks and probably have had more sexual partners than the average woman, but I have never seen a cock as great as Trent's. Its girth and length are absolutely perfect. Not so long that it'll hurt—bigger isn't always better, take it from me—but just long enough that I know he's going to feel fucking incredible.

Unable to stop myself, I reach out and grip it, sliding my hand up and down against the soft, velvety exterior of his hard length. He lets out a hiss and then grabs my wrist.

"I'm too close already. I need to be inside you."

I get up on my tiptoes and nip at his lip, eliciting another growl from him. "Then do it."

The words spark a fire in his eyes, and it's like I have unleashed a beast.

He walks me back until I fall onto the bed again and immediately drops to his knees and spreads my legs.

"Wait, I thought—" I don't get a chance to finish before his mouth is on my pussy, and he's sucking on my clit like his life depends on it. My body flushes with pleasure and I drop back, my hands gripping his hair as he takes me up higher and higher toward the peak of my orgasm.

He sticks a finger inside and curls it until he hits my G-spot, and that combined with his sucking motion on my clit sets off an explosive orgasm. I detonate, my whole body convulsing as bliss spreads throughout. My thighs clamp around his head as the orgasm carries on far longer than I'm used to, but he doesn't let up. If anything, it feels like he doubles down on his efforts.

I'm going to fucking pass out if he keeps this up.

I let out a scream as another orgasm rips through me on the tail end of my last one. He finally eases his ministrations and kisses my thighs before stopping completely and standing. I struggle to open my eyes, and when I see him wipe his hand across his mouth, which is wet from my release, I nearly come again at how sexy he looks.

He reaches down to his pants on the floor, grabs a condom from his pocket, and then puts it on. In the meantime, I somehow find the energy to scoot back on the bed. I hope he doesn't expect me to get on top because my legs are pretty useless right now.

The hunger in his gaze hasn't faded at all—if anything, he seems ravenous, his eyes a little wild with need. He climbs on top of me and kisses me fiercely. "Becka," he says my name like a prayer and my heart soars.

Forget falling.

I'm in love with him already.

Which seems totally crazy since it's only been a few weeks. But then again, maybe it's not. We've known each other so long. Maybe it was always supposed to be this easy between us. This simple to go from friends to lovers.

He slides inside me, and I know I've never felt anything as perfect as Trent Bridger. "Trent," I whisper, my voice a plea. "Don't stop."

He shakes his head and pumps harder, our gazes locked on each other. It feels intimate and vulnerable. I've never looked into the eyes of my lover while we were having sex. It's a little scary. I'm sure he can see everything I'm feeling, just like I can see what he's feeling.

Fortunately, it looks like we're feeling the same thing. He closes his eyes in bliss and lets out a groan. "Fuck, you feel too good. I'm not gonna last."

"Look at me." When he opens his eyes, I say, "Don't look away." I need to see his eyes. I need to know we're in this together. That this risk I took wasn't a mistake. This is big and scary, and I need to know I'm not going to be abandoned again.

His face gets serious, and I can tell he's fighting his release. He shifts slightly, and I let out a gasp. He's now rubbing on my overly sensitive clit with every thrust and, oh God, it feels so good.

"Trent…" I breathe out before I'm coming again, my legs shaking as the waves of pleasure wash over my body until I'm wrung out. He pumps once more and then shouts my name as he comes. His whole body shivers and then he drops his head to my chest, before gently pulling out and rolling to lie next to me, both of us breathless.

"I need to take care of the condom," he says and drops a kiss to my head before I feel the bed shift, but I can't look. My eyes are heavy, and my body feels weightless.

"Okay," I mumble as sleep overtakes me.

15

TRENT

What the fuck did I just do?

That was not supposed to happen. I scrub my scalp and stare at my reflection in Becka's bathroom while guilt pummels me.

I messed up. We were supposed to be just friends. How could I slip and mess up this badly? I haven't done something this dumb since my early days of fame.

No, that's not right. What just happened with Becka will never be something that I'll regret as much as I do some of my behavior in those early days of the band hitting it big. But this is still bad. Really, really bad.

I need her as my friend. I need her in my life. Have I just fucked that all up by having sex with her?

Mind-blowing sex at that. Fuck, no one has ever felt as good as Becka.

NO!

Fuck, I have to stop thinking about her like that. I need to get us back on the friendship track. As great as that was, it was a mistake. Friends with benefits always gets messy, and I know if we date and break up, she'll never speak to me again. The idea guts me even thinking about it.

I know she's going to be mad if I tell her we shouldn't do that again, but mad is temporary. She'll realize our friendship is more important.

I need her. I can't let sex ruin what we have. I've never felt as close to someone outside of the band as I do to Becka.

Okay, this is fine. I can fix this. I quickly wash my hands, and then go back into her room.

I stop in my tracks when I see her lying there, her chest moving with even breaths, her lips slightly parted, and a serene expression on her face. Fuck, she fell asleep.

I rub my head, trying to think about a plan B. How do I handle this and not make things worse? I'm in uncharted territory here. I consider leaving but quickly push that thought away. No, I need to be here when she wakes up.

And maybe there's a small part of me that wants to jump at the chance to hold her like this, intimately. Even if I know I can't keep her like this. *We need to stay friends.* I keep hoping the words will erase how good she felt beneath me, but they don't. If anything, the thought frustrates me because I know I'll never forget having her this way, but I need to do what's right for our friendship.

I gently lie back down in her bed, trying not to jostle her around. She immediately rolls toward me and curls up next to me, her hand resting on my chest and one of her legs lying across mine. I watch her sleep for hours, memorizing every line of her face, the few freckles that I've never noticed before that dot her nose. Eventually, my eyes droop, heavy from exhaustion, and I fade to sleep.

I wake up to bright light filling the room. Becka is asleep curled away from me. We aren't touching, but my body faces hers. I can't tell if she's awake yet, so I lift my head and try to look around her, but I'm still not sure.

"Becks," I whisper.

"Hmm," she mumbles. Then she quickly rolls over, her hand to her chest, and looks at me with wide eyes. "Oh shit, I thought it was a dream."

Oh, thank God. Maybe she won't be too mad at me after all.

Relief must show on my face because she gets a questioning look. "Trent?"

"Last night was crazy, right? I'm so glad we're on the same page. I was worried we messed up our friendship."

Her expression turns neutral, but she shifts so she's lying on her back and looking up at me as I rest my head on my hand. "You were worried?"

"Yeah, I mean sex usually changes things." I grab her hand and hold it tightly with mine. I stare at her earnestly, deciding I need to put it all on the line to make sure I smooth this over as much as possible. I'm desperate not to lose her. "I don't want anything to change with us, Becka. Your friendship means the world to me. You've given me something I didn't think I'd ever find again—someone who wants to know me, the real me. I don't want last night to ruin what we have."

Her face doesn't change, but her eyes bounce back and forth between mine. I wish I knew what she was thinking. The silence is killing me. My heart starts pounding heavily waiting for her to say something, anything.

"Becka?"

Her eyes get big and wide, but her face remains carefully blank, which seems weird for her. "Sorry. I guess I'm still waking up and a little slow." She turns away and goes to roll out of the bed but stops. Her cheeks flush bright pink, and she turns to me. "Um, I'm still naked under here." She pats the covers that I placed over her when I got back in bed last night.

"Oh, right. Sorry. Here, I'll cover my eyes."

"Thanks," she says, but her word sounds soft and hollow. Fuck, is she embarrassed? I don't want that either, but I also don't want to rock the boat any more than necessary. This is going better than I thought it would, so it's probably best that I don't say much more. I feel the bed shift and hear Becka opening and closing drawers while I keep my hand over my eyes. I'm tempted to peek, to get one last look at her beautiful body before it's gone from me for good. But I fight the urge because I don't want to make things more awkward.

She clears her throat. "You can look now."

I uncover my eyes to see her in a pair of baggy sweats and an oversized sweatshirt. It's like she's hiding her body from me, and I hate it, even though I have no right to feel that way. I wanted friendship and that's what she's giving me. I'm lucky she's not yelling at me for last night.

"I'm gonna go make some coffee. You're welcome to get dressed in here and head out whenever."

She walks out of the room, and I stare at her retreating back. Something feels off. I quickly get dressed and head to the kitchen where she's standing at the island counter, holding a steaming cup of coffee in her hands and staring unseeingly out the window on the other side of her open living room. Even from here, you can see the distant crash of waves. It really is a beautiful view, but I'm more interested in figuring out the woman in the room.

I approach her cautiously. "Hey. You okay?"

She turns to me and smiles, but it doesn't reach her eyes. "Yeah, just tired." She takes a sip of her coffee and looks away again.

She could be tired, but I feel like there's more. I pull my phone out of my pocket and look at the time. I see a couple of texts from Tristan and one from Miles and notice that I need to leave right now if I'm going to make it back to my place in time for our meeting with the tour manager Robbie lined up.

Fuck.

I'm reluctant to leave her, but I also can't just bail on a meeting. "I gotta head out."

She nods but doesn't make eye contact. "I figured."

I head for the door, turning back to her before I open it. "Are we okay? You know, after everything that happened last night?"

She looks at me, her face back to that carefully neutral expression I'm starting to hate. "Yeah, we're fine."

I stare at her for a long moment before nodding and walking out. I'm halfway to my house before I get the sinking feeling that she was lying to me.

16

Becka

I stare at the door that Trent just walked through. The click of the latch thunders in my head, and I rush over and throw the deadbolt ensuring he can't come back in. The second it's locked I slide to the floor and finally let the tears fall free. My shattered heart still pounds in my chest, but it hurts with every shaky breath I take.

How did my perfect night turn into my worst nightmare?

I replay the morning in my head. Waking up and seeing him still there. My dreams had been filled with him, memories of our night together so vivid, I'd convinced myself there was no way they could be real. Then, when I woke up, he was there. His handsome face staring down at me, and I thought, "wow, it wasn't a dream."

I was so relieved until he opened his big, stupid mouth. And then he ruined what would've been a perfect morning. He ripped my heart into pieces, and I don't even think he realizes it.

All that risk turned out not to be worth it after all.

My heart was not safe in his hands like I thought it would be. Now it's more broken than I ever remember it being. I lean my head back against the door and close my eyes against the brightness coming in through the windows. I normally love how sunny it is here, but today I just want the day to be as miserable as I am.

I allow myself to cry for an hour before I push myself up and walk to my shower on wobbly legs. I'm going to wash away every memory of last night. Every touch, every kiss, every look. I don't want to remember any of it.

In the shower, I scrub until my body is red and feels raw. Then I get out and move to my bedroom, ripping the sheets off my bed, stomping to my laundry closet, and shoving them into the washer.

But it's not enough. The room still smells like him.

Fine. I can fix that.

I grab my cleaning supplies under my kitchen sink and go to town, deep cleaning my bedroom like I never have before. By the time I'm done it doesn't even smell like me, let alone Trent. It smells like lemon. I can handle lemon.

When I go to put away the cleaning supplies, I notice that my hand is shaking. When I take stock of my body, I realize my stomach is also grumbling. A glance at the clock tells me it's well past lunch and I never had breakfast. I grab a granola bar and then stare at my fridge for dinner options, but nothing sounds good. I don't want to cook. I don't want to do anything. Now that my cleaning spree is done, I feel drained, like every ounce of energy and happiness has been zapped right out of me.

I grab my phone to order takeout and stop in my tracks when I see a text message from Trent. No. Not today. Ignoring it, I order a pizza and wait for it to be delivered.

I grab a glass of wine and curl up in my reading chair that faces out so I can watch the view when I'm not using it to get lost in a book. A book doesn't sound appealing right now, but neither does TV. Nothing sounds good. Nothing feels like it will fill the emptiness that Trent left behind this morning.

And suddenly it hits me—and hits me hard—what I'm feeling. Abandonment. Even if it doesn't make sense, because he's not technically abandoned me. He wants to be my friend.

But that's all he wants.

And it's not enough for me. I wanted more. I wanted him—all of him.

And for a perfect moment, I had him.

I can't go back to just being his friend. I can't pretend that I didn't fall in love with him. That he didn't make me feel things I've never felt before. No. I can't go back to that.

It shouldn't be hard to push him away. He leaves for tour in a few days, and he'll be busy with that and filming the documentary.

My face goes slack. Oh fuck. I knew that was a risk, but I shoved the thought aside when we kissed. But now the weight of my stupidity is hitting me with the force of a category five hurricane. I'll be organizing press interviews and all social media campaigns leading up to the premiere, which will require me to work very closely with Trent. I can delegate until the cows come home if I'm willing to risk my job, but being the lead on a project this huge could lead to a promotion. Work is the one place I actually feel confident in what I'm doing. I have my shit together at work. I can't risk that. I've already taken one giant risk and look how well that turned out.

I take a sip of my wine, my brain going a mile a minute to figure out how I'll handle being around him all the time for the duration of the previews and premiere, but then I realize that's a problem for another day. They'll be on tour for months and then add an extra month or two of editing before the documentary will even be ready. I've got time. Almost a year in fact.

By then hopefully I'll be more put-together and over him.

I can only hope.

17

TRENT

"Staring won't make her text you back faster."

I don't bother responding to Tristan's comment. I texted Becka yesterday, and she still hasn't responded, which isn't like her, and that sinking feeling in my gut gets worse.

"It's not like her to not text me back."

"Maybe she's busy."

She could be. I know she has a lot of responsibilities at work, and VibeTV has a lot of big original projects premiering here in the next few weeks. But she's always been busy at work. That never stopped her from texting me before.

I mean, hell, I'm busy too. We leave for tour in five days, and there are a million things to do before we go, and yet I'm staring at my phone like a lovesick teenage girl.

"You gonna tell me what happened?"

I glance up. "What do you mean?"

He gives me a look. "Cut the shit, Trent. It's me. I can tell something happened between you two. You've been acting like a fool in love for weeks."

"Becka and I are just friends." I hate the words, even as I know that's all we can ever be. I can't lose her. And yet, it feels like I'm losing her with every second that passes without a response from her. She's gone radio silent, and I'm not handling it well.

We were supposed to go right back to being friends. She seemed fine with it. I mean, she even woke up saying she thought it was a dream. I've replayed that morning countless times in my head in the past nearly forty-eight hours. And every time I replay it, it's that first moment that changes the trajectory of the rest of the day. I've imagined what it would've been like if I'd kissed her instead of telling her we should stay friends. That's always a dangerous road to go down because it makes me want a lot of things I can't have.

Mainly her. All of her. Every glorious inch of—no, I have got to stop thinking that way.

I look down at my phone again and silently beg her to text me back. A word, an emoji. Any-fucking-thing would be better than her silence.

I'd take her anger. Her grief. Her joy. But I can't take her silence.

"Maybe I should go over there and talk to her."

"Not a good idea, big bro."

"Why?" I ask, angry that he didn't even hesitate in his response. What the fuck would he know about Becka?

"If she's not texting you, then what makes you think she'll want to talk to you? We have a few more days in town before tour. Give her a little breathing room."

But what if she decides she doesn't need me? That she's better off not being in my life?

Deep down I know Tristan is right. If I crowd her, I'll lose her.

If I haven't already.

Anxious energy swirls in my body making me bounce on my toes. Normally Kasen is the hyped up one, but he's hungover from partying too hard last night. Tristan is cool and casual like always. Miles is fiddling with his drumsticks. His anxiety has been worse since we all opted for sobriety to support Kasen, and I had to pull him aside this morning to tell him to smoke some weed before he had an anxiety attack. He's refusing until we get to our first stop tonight and he can smoke away from Kase. Robbie is talking to our tour manager, discussing some final details, and Jolie has her camera glued to her hand taking candid shots of us as we prepare to load the tour bus. Every tour she designates herself our tour photographer. She's pretty good too. So good, I actually made sure that we were paying her.

She makes us all look good, so she deserves to get paid for her hard work, even if it's something she does because she enjoys it.

But none of that is why I'm anxious.

I texted Becka last night asking her to come see us off. I confessed that I needed to see her before I go. I wanted to tell her I missed her, but I felt like that might be pushing it. She hasn't responded to any of my texts all week, and I'm going out of my fucking mind.

I even caved and went to her condo one night, but she wasn't there, which sent me on a completely different type of spiral.

Was she with another guy?

If she was, what right did I have to be upset with that?

But I was.

Fuck, I still am.

I don't know how this got all messed up. Okay, well maybe I kind of do. Part of me thinks it got messed up when we had sex, but deep down I know it wasn't sex that messed things up. The sex was perfect.

No one has ever had better sex than we did.

No, it was the morning after.

It was my fear of losing her.

And I've lost her anyway.

I know it deep in my heart. I have tried to deny the truth for as long as possible, but as the clock ticks closer to our departure time and she still doesn't show up, I know it for sure. Until finally, it's time. Robbie and Jolie get in first, followed by Kasen, then Miles, until it's just me and Tristan. I look down the road, staring and begging for her car to appear on the horizon, but it remains empty.

She's really not coming.

Tristan claps his hand on my shoulder and gives a squeeze. "Come on, Trent."

"Just another minute."

"She's not coming. Another minute won't change that."

His words punch me in the gut, and emotion clogs my throat. Disappointment. Regret. Heartbreak.

I can't leave her. Not with things like this between us. But what choice do I have? With one more glance down the road, I finally give up and get on the bus.

But my heart? My heart stays right there, shattered on the sidewalk.

18

Becka

ONE MONTH LATER

"Becka, do you have that report for Marshall?"

I glance up from my computer where I'm looking over the latest reviews of our original series to see what I can pull for advertising quotes. Simone stands at my door.

"Yeah, they're right here." I grab the requested reports and hand them to her.

She briefly looks them over. "You're a godsend. These look great. Thanks." She turns to leave but then turns back. "Have you started any of the preliminary market research on the Rapturous Intent documentary? We're hoping it'll be as successful as the Taylor Swift or Jonas Brothers docs. Marshall's getting nervous that maybe we're losing our window."

"Marshall worries too much."

She smiles at that and lifts her eyebrows in agreement.

"I've got Riley on it while I wrap up a couple of other projects. He feels confident it'll be one of our biggest premieres to date."

Simone lets out a relieved sigh. "Thank God. I didn't want to go to Marshall with bad news."

I paste a smile on my face. "No bad news here. Rapturous Intent is hotter than ever."

Simone gives me a thumbs-up and a wave and then leaves. At her departure, I sag in my chair and rub my chest, that nuisance called my heart aching relentlessly.

I can't wait for this fucking documentary to be over so I never have to think about Rapturous Intent again. It's like constantly rubbing salt in my open wound, and it's a painful reminder of what I can't have.

I rub my neck, hoping to ease the tension there, and then get back to work. I've been working overtime in an attempt to avoid thinking about Trent, even though work isn't exactly the best way to forget about him when my boss asks me about his band every other second.

Okay, maybe that's an exaggeration.

Whatever.

I'm angry and maybe a little bitter.

Hours later, I blink from my computer and realize it's gotten darker outside, and almost everyone else is gone. I head to the gym to get a workout in—my other attempt at keeping my mind off Trent.

Nighttime is the hardest time of day. When I'm home trying to relax and de-stress after a long day, that's when thoughts of Trent sneak in. And even though I removed every trace that he'd ever been there, whenever I lie in bed, all I can think about is how his body felt on top of mine. How he moved inside of me. How he looked into my eyes and I let him see into my soul while he made me feel a bliss I'd never known before.

I decided I needed to be so mentally and physically exhausted every night that I pass out basically the second I fall into bed. So I work until my brain is mush and then I go to the gym and work out until my muscles are shaking. Then I go home, take a shower, and fall into bed.

It's not a perfect plan, and I feel more drained than rejuvenated, but I've never been in better shape, and my boss is so impressed with my work ethic that she's considering me for a promotion even without my work on the Rapturous Intent documentary.

So, there's that at least.

When I get to the gym, my phone rings, and my mom's name flashes on the screen. "Hey, Mom, what's up?"

"Hey, hun. I wanted to check in with you. Lainey said you were working yourself to the bone."

"Well, isn't Lainey a giant tattletale."

"Oh stop," my mom lightheartedly chastises. "You know she has good intentions. Sometimes you just need your mom. It's not a bad thing, Becks. Lord knows, I've needed you kids more times than I can count. So, you gonna tell me what's going on? Or do I need to ask Will?"

"Ha! Joke's on you. Will doesn't know."

"Ah, so there is something going on."

Shit.

"You suck sometimes."

She laughs, and I miss her so much right now, I can hardly breathe. I lean against the wall of the locker room and try to take a breath, tears burning the backs of my eyes. She's right, sometimes a girl just needs her mom.

I nibble my lip and confess, "I might be a little heartbroken."

"Tell me about him."

And with those words, the dam breaks. I've been proudly holding myself together since that first morning where I cried after Trent left. I haven't shed a tear since, but confessing everything to my mom tells me maybe I haven't been dealing with everything after all—more like avoiding.

I'm incredibly thankful there's no one else in the women's locker room because I probably look like a fucking basket case. It takes a while to tell my mom all about running into Trent again after what happened with Brad—who now feels like a complete nobody compared to Trent. I leave out the details of our night together, for obvious reasons. When I'm done, I grab the box of

Kleenex off the counter and blow my nose. I chance a peek in the mirror and nearly groan with how awful I look. My face is red and blotchy, and my eyes are already swelling from how hard I cried. My nose looks like I'm competing with Rudolph the reindeer and is still slightly runny.

I look like a hot mess.

But I feel a little better. Like finally talking about him allowed me to heal a little bit.

"Why didn't you tell him you didn't think it was a mistake?"

"Because he made it super clear he just wanted to be my friend and that was important to him."

"But you said you haven't talked to him since."

"Correct."

"So, now he doesn't even have you as a friend."

I never thought about it that way. I've been so wrapped up in my hurt, I never took the time to think about how Trent would be feeling. How ignoring him might've hurt him.

At the time, I had to ignore him for my sanity. I couldn't be around him after our night together and not be hurt that he didn't want more with me.

"I guess you're right."

"Now, it's been a long time since I've seen Trent, and I'm sure he's changed a lot."

"Not that much," I tell her. "He's surprisingly down-to-earth still."

"Do you think it's possible he was feeling more too, but didn't want to lose you?"

"How would he lose me if we were more?" I exclaim. "We'd be a couple! He'd have me all the time, as friend and girlfriend. Wouldn't that be the best of both worlds?"

"But what if things ended? I'm not saying they would, but no relationship comes with a guarantee. What if you risked your friendship for a relationship that turned sour down the road and then you had nothing?"

"We have nothing now!"

My mom remains calm, even as I start to get louder. "I understand that, but look at things from another perspective. I'm actually surprised you didn't talk to Will about this. Men process issues differently than women, sweetie, even if we don't want them to. Raising a son gave me better insight into that, but Doug has really made me realize how different men and women think, sometimes even about the simplest things. Maybe you should try talking to Trent. You said he still occasionally texts you."

At least once a week, I get a text from him. Sometimes, he tells me a story from the road. Other times he just asks how I'm doing. But every week, without fail, he attempts to contact me. "Yeah."

"Well, maybe next time text him back. You won't get any answers by shutting down, Becka. You have to communicate with him."

God, that's so much easier said than done. It's so much easier just to ignore him and run away from my problems.

"Becka?"

"Yeah, I heard you, Mom." And I did. But I still don't know if I'm strong enough to talk to him. What if talking makes things worse?

The truth is, I'm afraid of what I feel for him and how badly he could crush me. I need to get thicker skin before I talk to him again. I need to know that he won't break me.

But as time goes on, I wonder if I'll ever get to that point, or if I've fallen too far anyway.

19

TRENT

TWO MONTHS LATER

Sometimes silence is louder than words. My brother told me that after Becka's first month of radio silence. Now two months later, the words cycle through my head every time I send a text that goes unanswered. But like the fool that I am, I still send her a message every week.

In some selfish way, it makes me feel like at the very least she can't forget me.

Unless of course she's blocked me, but I don't think she has. I hope she hasn't.

Robbie pops into the backstage area where we're getting ready. "Y'all set for the film crew?"

Tristan nods, and Robbie sends them in. A normal tour is hard enough, but adding a film crew to it has added an extra layer of pressure. Not to mention the fact that I haven't quite been myself. Normally, I play up the rock star persona on tour. It's what people expect, and I've never really had a problem with it before. The band knows who I am.

But Becka's going to see this footage, and the idea of her seeing me flirt with other women makes me sick to my stomach.

So instead, I've been myself, which is terrifying in its own right. Miles and Tristan have been keeping an eye on me, neither ever letting me be alone for too long. Kasen is in his own world, which is concerning in itself. More and more, he's acting like he did when he was using before. So the fact that Miles and Tris have to split their time babysitting the two of us makes me feel like shit.

I'm supposed to be the papa bear. I'm supposed to hold everyone else together, not be the one who falls apart. But lately, I feel like my foundation is crumbling. I'm writing killer songs, so at least there's some small semblance of a silver lining, but it doesn't make up for the void that Becka left inside me.

I'd give anything to change how that morning turned out, but there's nothing I can do to fix it now, especially not when we're on the road for the next several months. So, now I just settle for feeling lost.

The camera crew comes in, and Fletcher, the creator and director, gets set up. He's interviewing Kasen tonight, and I've never been so grateful not to have the spotlight on me. I need a night off. We've been going nonstop, and it's wearing me down more than it ever has before.

I'm exhausted. Mentally, physically, emotionally.

We all do our preshow routines while Kasen does his interview and then head out to the stage. The bright lights hit me, and I instantly feel their heat across my skin. I grip the mic in my hand and hold it to my mouth, hearing my breath echo across the stadium as our fans screams die down until it's so quiet, I can hear when the guy in the back coughs. Tristan plays the opening chords, then I open my mouth, pouring my heart—or what's left of it—into the lyrics until I'm lost to the sea of faceless fans before me. But there's no high this time. The adrenaline that usually courses through my veins isn't there. I feed off the energy of the crowd just to get through the show, but it's not my best performance. I doubt anyone out in the crowd noticed, but I do.

The show finally comes to an end, and we leave the stage, the roar of the crowd behind us until we're so far backstage we can't hear them anymore. I'm lost in a daze as I quickly shower and then escape the craziness of our band dressing room, where groupies are already hanging on Kasen and Miles. I sneak out the side door, hoping to get out before anyone sees me. The cab I called is already here and waiting for me, but before I can slide in, Tristan shows up behind me. "Thought you could use some company tonight."

I frown, but I'm too tired to fight him on this. I want to be alone, but maybe I shouldn't be.

Without a word, I get in the cab with Tristan right on my heels. We ride in silence to the park I found online and then walk to the swing set. Again, he doesn't speak and neither do I. He just lets me do my thing.

I kick hard, pushing myself higher and higher, and then throw my body off, but instead of landing on my feet like I always do, I overshoot and land in a pile of limbs.

"Trent!"

I groan as I roll over. Everything hurts. My heart, my mind, and now my body.

But maybe I deserve this.

Tristan rushes over to me. "Shit. Are you okay?"

"Yeah. Nothing's broken." But I don't move. I just lie there. "I fucked it up, Tris." Tears fill my eyes. "I miss her so damn much."

He sits down and leans his arms over his bent knees. "I know you do."

"I want her back. I want to go back to that morning and not fuck it all up."

"You can't go back, no matter how badly you want to." There's a wistfulness and regret in his voice, and I look over at him, noticing how sad his face is as his mind clearly wanders back in time. He's never told me the full story about what happened with Jolie and how she ended up with Robbie instead of him.

"Will you tell me what happened with you and Jolie?"

He looks at me then and shakes his head. "It won't make any difference, so there's no point talking about it."

I look at my brother and can't help but wonder if that's what I'll be like if I never get Becka back. Will I always wonder what could've been? Will my life be filled with meaningless hookups because I can't have the one woman I want?

But there's a big difference between my brother and me. He lost his chance with Jolie because she married someone else. As far as I know, Becka is still single.

Which means I still have a chance to make this right.

20

Becka

The smell of maple and bacon wafts through the air, and my stomach gurgles in complaint that I still haven't eaten.

"Fuck, that French toast looks divine," Gwen says from beside me as our waitress places a plate in front of me. The eggy bread is drenched in butter, syrup, and powdered sugar, and I can't wait to eat every last bite.

The waitress drops off the rest of the plates, and we all dive in. Clearly we were all hungry because silence reigns supreme as we eat, and it isn't until most of us are halfway finished that Beth finally puts her fork down, clasps her hands on the table, and stares at each of us in turn.

"Are we finally going to address the elephant at the table, or are we still pretending it's not there?"

My brows furrow in confusion, and I wait for her to elaborate. She looks pointedly at Gwen and then Lainey before staring me down. "We know something's going on with you. Lainey won't tell us what it is, but it's obvious to anyone who knows you that you aren't okay."

My cheeks flood pink with embarrassment. Have I been that obvious? I know I should've told them sooner about Trent. I mean, hell, these women are my best friends. But the truth was I needed time to sort out my feelings. Although I don't know if I've done much sorting. It's still more avoiding than anything else. But clearly I can't keep it from them any longer.

I glance at Lainey and give her a silent thank you with my eyes. She knows some of what's going on. Not a ton of details, but enough to know it's about a guy, and Trent in particular.

"I was seeing someone, well sorta not really. It's complicated."

"Do we need to beat him up? If you need our help burying a body, I just need to stop by a hardware store and buy a shovel and some rose bushes," Gwen says.

"Why rose bushes?" Beth asks.

"So the police won't be on to us. I can't just buy a shovel—that's obviously sketchy—but if I buy a shovel so I can plant the rose bushes, then I'm all good."

"That is strangely logical," Beth responds while I fight against the urge to laugh at Gwen.

"No burying of bodies will be necessary. It wasn't like that. We were friends, we crossed a line, and now we're nothing." My voice catches on the last word, belying my statement.

Although it's the truth. We aren't anything anymore. I know it's my fault. We could've stayed friends if I could get over my hurt, but I just can't. Maybe in time. Maybe years from now after I've met someone else, the memory of Trent won't weigh quite so heavily on my heart.

But now is not that time. Especially since even the idea of a future with someone else makes my heart hurt so painfully in my chest, I'm convinced this must be early signs of a heart attack.

"We're worried about you," Gwen says gently from beside me. She places her hand on my arm and gives me a soft, caring smile. "You're working crazy hours, and while you look great physically, you have dark bags under your eyes, and you rarely smile anymore."

"I smile," I say and glance over to Lainey so she can back me up, but I'm only met with her sympathetic gaze.

"You haven't smiled at these brunches in months," Lainey says, her voice soft like she's trying to soothe a sick puppy.

That can't be right. I smile all the time. Don't I?

Beth and Gwen sit in their chairs both looking a little nervous and a lot worried. God, I've been such a shit friend lately. "I'm sorry. I didn't realize."

"It's okay. We're just worried about you. Will you tell us what's going on?"

Reluctantly, I do. It's easier telling them the story than it was telling my mom, probably since more time has passed and it doesn't feel quite as fresh, even if the pain still lingers. By the time I'm done, both Gwen and Beth have tears in their eyes on my behalf, and Lainey watches me with a thoughtful expression on her face.

"I'm so sorry you've been dealing with this all by yourself, Becka," Beth says.

"It's okay. I think I needed to process it for a while before I talked about it. I'm sorry I kept it from you guys."

"We get it. Heartbreak sucks. That offer to bury him if you need it still stands. I don't care how famous he is," Gwen says, causing us all to burst into a fit of laughter.

"There it is," Gwen says with a wide smile.

"What?" I ask her.

"Your smile. It's been a long time since we've seen it." I feel the pull of my cheeks and realize she's right. I'm smiling, and my cheeks feel stretched like they haven't smiled this wide in a long time.

"Thank you," I tell her softly.

We wrap up brunch, and Gwen and Beth head their separate ways. Lainey walks with me to my car since hers is parked near mine. She didn't speak much at brunch, and I'm wondering what her thoughts are on all of this.

"So, you got any advice for me, oh, wise older sister?"

She stares at the street in front of us. "Did I ever tell you what happened between me and Owen?"

"Owen Bishop? No, you didn't."

"Mmhmm," she smiles faintly, though it doesn't reach her eyes, before her gaze drops to the sidewalk. "He was the first boy I ever loved, and probably the best thing I've ever had. I used to laugh at the mean girls at school because I knew they were going to peak in high school while I had my whole life in front of me. I was going to get out of Texas and do something important. Then I fell for a boy whose family is so embedded in our small town that it's named after them. A boy whose entire future was rooted in that small town."

She faces me, and her eyes are a little manic. "I knew what my future held if I stayed, so I chose to leave because I wanted to do more. I went to UT and expected him to stay in Bishop Ridge and work for his dad, but he followed me. We stayed together all through college, and when we graduated, he proposed."

"Wait, what?! How did I not know this?"

Her eyes get teary, and her voice gets hoarse as she explains, "Because I turned him down. I told everyone we broke up because we wanted different things, but that was only partially true. He wanted to marry me and start a family, and while I loved him and wanted those things too, I didn't want them in Bishop Ridge, and his dad was pressuring him to come home and take over the family business. I knew if I asked him to come with me instead of moving back home, he would, but at what cost? And all I could think was that someday he'd come to resent me, or worse, leave me. So I let him go."

Tears stream quietly down her face one at a time, and she grips both my upper arms forcing me to look at her. "I let my own insecurities ruin the best thing I've ever had and the truest love I've ever known. I don't want that for you, Becks. Talk to Trent. Clear the air before it really, truly is too late. I don't want you to live with the same kind of regrets that I do."

My heart breaks for all the pain my sister has quietly endured, and my own tears fall down my face as we hug each other on the middle of a sidewalk in Santa Monica.

For two women who don't cry that much, we're doing an awful lot of crying, but her words keep ricocheting in my head, and I know she's right. I need to do something.

The problem is I'm scared, and every time I've attempted to respond to one of his texts, I freeze. It's like my entire body shuts down, unable to do anything until I put the phone down.

It's later that night when I'm lying in bed, begging my brain to stop thinking about Trent so I can finally go to sleep, when I remember something Lainey said to me. She let Owen go before he could leave her.

My past filters through my mind like a movie, each boyfriend or romantic encounter being seen for the first time with a new lens. How many times have I dumped a guy before he could dump me? And regardless of who dumped who, I always acted like they were dead to me the moment we were done. Even with Brad. I ignored him for weeks, only interacting with him at work if I was forced to, but he might as well have been a nameless temp for all I cared at that point.

Am I doing the same thing—to a different degree—with Trent?

The realization settles deep in my bones as I realize I might need professional help to get over this one.

21

BECKA

THREE MONTHS LATER

It's been six months since that night with Trent, and I wish I could say that I'm over him. That he didn't leave a giant void inside me, but the truth is I miss him more every day. Therapy hasn't helped me in the way I thought it would. Don't get me wrong, it's working, but it's a painstakingly slow process. Each session we get closer to battling the demons that still have me freezing up whenever I try to text Trent, but the progress has been slower than I expected, and I find myself asking more questions than getting answers.

What hasn't changed at all is that I still feel like a giant piece of my heart is missing. I didn't just lose the man I'd fallen for, I lost my friend. It was always so easy with Trent. We could talk for hours about nothing and everything. We enjoyed watching the same movies and listening to all different types of music. Spending time with him took me back to all those times we'd hang out as kids and preteens. The long hot Texas days, chasing fireflies, making mud pies.

It was a simpler time.

Part of me understands why he was so eager to get back to

being friends. I know what that meant to him. I can't imagine the life he's lived as a rock star, but it does seem pretty superficial.

But another part of me can't let go of the fact that he thought our night together was a mistake.

I thought it was perfect.

But I guess I was alone in that. I let out a heavy sigh and then grab another chocolate chip cookie. I'll work out tomorrow, but tonight I've decided to wallow. I've been holding myself together for the past few months—barely, but still. I go out with my friends, I laugh, I smile. I go to work, then the gym, never diverting from what has turned into a robotic schedule. I pretend I'm not still aching for him.

I think I deserve a night of being sad and lonely. Tucking my feet under me on my couch, I dip my cookie in my glass of milk, my eyes glued to the TV screen and a different pair of piercing blue eyes than the ones I dream about. My phone rings, and I glance down to where it sits on the armrest.

I put down my milk glass and slide the accept button. "Hey, Elise, what's up?"

"Hey, Mom wanted me to call and check up on you."

I can't help but smile. "Way to rat her out."

Elise just laughs, "Come on, you know how she can be. She worries about us."

"Yeah, she does."

"So...how are you?"

I let out a heavy breath, trying to figure out how to answer. I really don't know. Some days I feel okay, other days, every little thing makes me think of him, and it feels like someone is trying to take my heart out with a sharp knife. Today I just feel weighed down with sadness, my whole body bearing the weight of my heartbreak.

"I'm fine." It's not true now, but someday it will be.

"I call bullshit."

"No, really, I'm fine."

"Uh-huh." She pauses, and I nibble on my cookie while I wait for her to say something else. "I can hear *The Great British Baking Show* in the background. How many times are you going to watch that show?"

"Shut up, Elise. The tent is my happy place. Leave me alone."

She has the audacity to laugh, I'm pretty sure at me. "It's your dead giveaway. You only watch that when you are depressed."

"I do not!"

"When Will got engaged to Candace and you guys got in that huge fight and you swore you were going to lose him—you watched it. When Sterling Maxwell cheated on you—you watched it. When Brad broke things off and you said you were totally fine because it was just a little break, but really you were super sad? You watched—"

"Okay, you've made your point."

She sounds smug, and I can just imagine the shit-eating grin she's wearing. Little sisters. "So, you gonna tell me how you really are now?"

I rub my eyes and lean back against my couch. "I don't know. I really don't. So I can't give you a solid answer."

"How about how you're doing right this minute?"

"I'm sad. I..." My eyes well with tears—another unexpected side effect of therapy now that I'm constantly asked to evaluate my feelings—and I take a minute to catch my breath. As I attempt to work through my shit, I know I am crying more than I probably have in my entire life. "I miss him. I miss our friendship too."

"Is he still texting you?"

"Yeah." Every week like clockwork. I still don't respond, but it's no longer because I don't want to. It's more that I'm still frozen and don't know what to say. So much time has passed. That night changed things between us, and I can't go back, but I also miss him with a fierceness that makes my body physically ache.

"Maybe one of these days you should text him back."

"And say what?"

"What you just told me—that you miss him."

I sigh, tired of thinking about him and this stupid mess we've put ourselves in. "What good would that do? It doesn't change anything. He doesn't want us to be more than friends. He made that clear. And I don't know that I can go back to just friends."

I've often wondered if maybe the sex wasn't as good for him. He said it was, but that was in the heat of the moment, and I know he's more experienced than I am. Maybe what I thought was perfect was just okay for him.

God, that's mortifying. Here I've been super stubborn about not talking to him, and he's probably just trying to figure out why I'm so upset over mediocre sex.

I wish it had been mediocre for me.

"I hate knowing you're so heartbroken," Elise says.

"Yeah, well, I hate being heartbroken. In fact, tell me something happy so I don't think about my own problems for five minutes."

"I passed my GRE and will officially be pursuing grad school."

"What?! No way! I'm so proud of you!"

"Thanks. I was super nervous about it, and now I'm just glad that part's over. I hate tests."

"I know you do." Elise has massive testing anxiety, and she's had to fight hard to overcome it so she can pursue her dream of becoming a veterinarian.

"Any other news I should be aware of?" I ask her.

"Um..."

"What? What is it?"

"I'm looking for Dad."

I swear my jaw drops to the floor. "What?"

She huffs out an exasperated sigh. I'm guessing she's already talked to Mom or Lainey about this too and is expecting me to tell her that it has bad idea written all over it, like I'm sure they have. "I want to know, okay? I want to know what happened to him. Where he went. What he's been doing for the past twenty-two years."

No, she wants to know why he left us. And I can't blame her.

It's the reason I reached out to him so long ago, and I can't lie and say the thought hasn't crossed my mind to try again now that I'm in therapy.

Lainey, Will, and I have all mostly moved on. Well, apart from our apparent abandonment issues. But we gave up on trying to find him or even bothering to think much about him at all after he contacted Will when he was drafted to the NFL. Will knows more about what he was doing with his life at that point, but Lainey and I didn't want to know. The fact he came out of the rock he crawled under just to tie himself to Will's fame disgusted us.

"What did Mom say when you talked to her about this?"

"That it was a bad idea and he wasn't a good guy, which is kind of obvious. If he was a good guy, he wouldn't have left his wife with four kids under seven years old. But I need to know."

"I get it."

"Don't try to—wait, did you say you get it?"

"Yeah."

She lets out a breath. "Wow, I thought you were going to try to talk me out of it like Mom and Lainey did."

"Nope. Have you had any luck finding him?"

"Not yet. I just started my search. Do you want to know if I find him?"

I shouldn't because I know in my gut that it's likely nothing good will come from that conversation, but what if he can finally give me some of the answers I need to get closure?

"Yeah, I think I do."

"Okay. I'll keep you posted."

We hang up shortly after, but instead of feeling settled and calm like I normally do after talking to my sister, my chest feels tight like it's hard to breathe. I can't tell which part of our conversation is bothering me more—the part where she's trying to find our deadbeat dad, or the part where she told me I should talk to Trent. Everyone in my family thinks I should talk to Trent. Well, everyone except Will. I never told him what happened between us. He's got his own shit to deal with. I didn't want to put my crap on him too.

The problem is I'm a coward.

I always thought I was brave and fierce, but these past few months have shown me how not brave I really am. I'm too chicken to talk to Trent. I'm afraid he'll tell me he still only wants to be friends. I'm afraid he'll tell me he loves me. I'm afraid he'll tell me he never wants to talk to me again.

I'm just…afraid of it all.

And until I know how to conquer that fear, his texts will have to remain unanswered.

22

TRENT

TWO MONTHS LATER

It feels good to be back in LA again. This was our longest tour, and I know we're all ready to be home. Mainly I'm just ready to finally be back in the same city as Becka. She can't ignore me anymore if I sit in front of her door until she opens it the fuck up.

I've had eight months to think about what I would say to her if she answered my texts, how I wouldn't waste my chance with her.

I've already made that mistake. I won't make it again.

But the key to my plan is to talk to her. I have to talk to her. I could've called her while we were on the road, but the thought that she might answer and I couldn't just go over to her house after we worked through things made me feel antsy. I want to be near her when we work things out, so I can finally kiss her again like I've been dying to.

But first, we have our final show of the tour, and more importantly, Will is going to be here with his new girlfriend, Gina. I'm happy for him. He's been alone for a long time since his fiancée died, and no one deserves happiness more than he does.

But it's going to be damn hard to see him when I'm in love

with his sister. I wonder if he knows about our falling-out? Has she talked to him about me? Or has she remained silent?

I don't know which scenario worries me more. But either way, it'll be good to see Will.

I walk down the hall toward my dressing room when I hear my name shouted behind me. I turn around at the familiar voice and feel my cheeks lift high in a wide smile. "Will! Damn, man, it's good to see you!" And it is, even if it breaks my heart a little bit when I realize he doesn't look at me any differently. He doesn't know about me and Becka then. I paste my smile on my face, already embracing my rock star persona and hoping he can't see the cracks.

I head toward him, and we give each other a one-armed hug.

"It's good to see you too, man. This is my girlfriend, Gina."

I glance at the beautiful woman next to him with golden skin and honey-brown eyes. Her dark hair flows in waves past her shoulders, and she wears a pair of dark skinny jeans and a deep red top. She's staring at Will, a questioning look on her face, and they have a silent conversation like couples tend to do before her lips tilt up into a radiant smile.

I'd find her absolutely stunning if I wasn't completely enamored with Becka. No one measures up to her.

"H...Hi." She giggles, and it's the familiar starstruck giggle I'm used to getting from fans.

I pull her into a hug. "Any girl of Will's is a friend of mine. Nice to meet you. It's been a long time since Will's had a girlfriend, so you must be someone special."

She giggles again nervously, and Will snorts at her reaction. I fight back my own smile. She'll have to learn to get used to me if I work things out with Becka because then I'll be hanging out with Will a lot more when I'm in town.

Will watches the hustle and bustle that is the norm backstage and gives me a look filled with admiration and pride. "You really did it."

I can't help feeling proud, even if this last tour was harder on me than any ever have been before. "Yeah. Some days I can't believe this is my life. But I bet you know how it is."

"Yeah, I can definitely relate."

"I'd love to catch a game next time we're in town." I haven't watched Will play football since high school. It would be great to see him play again.

"I'll hook you up. Just text me."

"Will do. You two gonna be around after? I gotta finish up my preshow ritual, but I'd love to catch up more."

I don't have a preshow ritual. I'm just feeling my cracks get a little wider, and I know I won't be able to stand here much longer without asking about Becka.

Both of us look to Gina who's staring at me, eyes wide, jaw open, in shock. Will chuckles and then says, "Yeah, we'll be here."

I glance at him, then Gina, then back at him before leaning forward and whispering to him conspiratorially, "I get that a lot. Don't worry, I won't steal your girl."

Just your sister.

He pulls Gina closer against him, and jealousy spikes through me like a lance because I want that—I want to be able to hold Becka close to me and be that possessive of her. "I'd fight for her, so you wouldn't stand a chance."

I smile at him, understanding better than he even realizes. I have my own girl I'm about to fight like hell for.

I get it.

Without another word, I pat him on the back and then head to my dressing room. I'm more determined than ever to make things right with Becka, and I think I just found my opening.

The after-party is already in full swing by the time we show up. Instead of joining everyone else, I sneak away upstairs and call the one person I've been dying to talk to for the past eight months.

The phone rings so many times, I'm convinced she's not going to answer. My whole body is strung tight like one of my guitar strings, but I refuse to hang up until she sends me to voice mail.

Come on, Becka. Answer the phone.

Then it stops and there's silence. I check the phone and see the time of the call going up. She answered.

"Becka?"

When she still doesn't say anything, I say, "I saw your brother."

She's silent on the other end of the phone, but I can hear her quietly breathing.

"How've you been?" I wait, the minutes stretching out before me like all the miles that have been between us the past eight months while I was on tour. Still, she says nothing, but she also doesn't hang up.

My eyes close, and on a soft breath I admit, "I miss you, Becka."

A shuddering breath travels through the line. "I'm sorry. I can't do this, Trent," she whispers, her voice hoarse and thick like she's fighting back tears.

My chest tightens, and a sense of urgency overwhelms me, like if she hangs up, then that'll be it. I'll have lost her for good.

"Becka—" Before I've even finished the word, the line goes dead, and with it my hopes for salvaging my relationship with her.

I drop my hand from my face, the phone still clutched in my palm weighing it down. The sounds of the party filter into the room, and I turn just in time to see Tristan pop his head in.

"Hey, what are you doing in here? Are you actually hiding during a party in our honor?"

His smile falls as he looks me over, his eyes locking on the phone in my hand at my side. His gaze shoots back up to mine, and he steps fully into the room, closing the door behind him and silencing the rambunctious noise from the party. "Did you call her?"

I nod, still struggling to find my voice when all my energy seems to be focused on stopping the internal bleeding. That's what happens when your heart's ripped out, right? Even if it's your own damn fault.

"What'd she say?"

I shake my head, fighting back my own emotions. I can't lose her. She was struggling. That has to mean she's not over me, right?

I stand up, a burst of energy shooting through me and that sense of urgency spreading like wildfire. "I have to go see her."

Tristan blocks my path. "Okay, hold on a sec. What happened? What'd she say?"

I shake my head and run my hand over my head, my eyes looking everywhere around the room, unable to settle on any one spot while I try to come up with a plan.

"Trent."

"She hardly said anything. She said she couldn't do this, but she sounded like she was on the verge of tears." I look at him, and he must see my desperation because he nods and says, "Okay, let's go over to her place. I'm coming with you."

I nod my head. "I don't care if the whole band comes as long as I get over there tonight. I have to see her."

We head back through the party and straight out to Tristan's car. He turns on the car, but before we even have a chance to pull away, my aunt's name flashes on his display as a call comes through the Bluetooth.

"Why would Aunt Jenny be calling this late? It's gotta be nearly three a.m. in Texas," Tristan asks aloud and then accepts the call.

"Hey, everything okay?"

"Tris, do you know where Trent is?"

Tristan and I both look at each other, our brows furrowed in concern. "I'm right here. What's going on?"

"It's Ted. He's had a heart attack." Her voice breaks, and she takes a minute to compose herself. I lean my elbow on the window and put my hand against my head as reality comes crashing down around me.

Once again, I'm getting pulled away from Becka before I have a chance to fix things. But my aunt and uncle are the only family Tristan and I have left. So as much as it guts me, I start looking up flight information and texting Miles, Kasen, and Robbie. I find us a flight out in a few hours, which gives us just enough time to head straight to LAX.

As the plane pulls away from the ground, I look out the window watching LA fading away and knowing my heart is down there somewhere with someone who doesn't even know it belongs to her.

23

Becka

My phone feels heavy as I hold it against my chest and let out a sob. God, hearing his voice was both the best feeling in the world and incredibly painful.

He misses me, but I didn't even have the strength to ask if he missed me as only a friend or as more.

Does he miss me how I miss him?

Or does he just miss his friend from Texas who knew him before he was a rock star?

Does it even matter?

For eight months, I've thought about Trent every day, and the more time that passed the more I wondered if it's better that things fell apart. If we got together, how long would we even last? I know myself well enough to know I need a man who's here, who's present when I need him, not someone who will be on the road half the year or more touring and having women constantly throwing themselves at him.

God, the idea makes my stomach curdle.

I lie back in my bed and throw the covers over my head, wanting to drown out the world and my heartache. Shouldn't this have faded by now? Why is this such a persistent ache? I was able to get over Brad in no time at all, and we actually dated for nine months.

Why can't I get over Trent when we only had one night together?

My mind races with questions, my heart aches with pain, and my body lies heavy on my bed until a fitful sleep finally overcomes it all.

My brother's huge smile consumes his face, and he looks as excited as a little kid on Christmas at how well his new girlfriend, Gina, and I are getting along. I found out he met her family a week ago, so of course, I demanded to meet her. It took him nearly a week to finally schedule something, and I admit I was a mess of nerves when I drove to the dog park.

Will doesn't have the best track record when it comes to choosing good women. Well, I guess it's only one woman since Gina is only his second serious relationship. But after Candace, I'm especially protective when it comes to my brother. Which is also why I still haven't told him about Trent calling me two weeks ago. I haven't heard a word from him since.

Not a text.

Not a call.

Nothing.

And I'm fucking gutted at his silence.

Is this how he felt all those months that I ignored his texts? Even if I pored over them nightly, reading and rereading them and torturing myself, he didn't know that. I don't know what his silence means, but it can't be anything good.

But Will is finally happy, and I don't want to ruin that.

Now if Gina turns out to be a bitch, it'll be a completely different story. I'm sick of gold diggers trying to own my brother.

I see Rex, Will's dog, pouncing around my brother and a beautiful woman whose curves are envy-inducing. She looks nothing like Candace, and a small bit of relief courses through me. Now I can only hope her personality is nothing like Candace too.

"Rex! Come here, boy," I shout, and Rex immediately comes bounding over to me. God, I love this fucking dog so much. I usually have him stay with me when Will's out of town for away games, and he's made these past eight months a little more bearable. There's a reason they call dogs man's best friend—they're empathetic, caring, and sometimes feel like people in their own right.

Honestly dogs are better than people.

I give Rex a scratch behind his ears and then walk toward my brother. Gina looks nervous, and that endears her to me even more, so I decide to go into this as friendly as possible. I give her a kind smile and then walk right up to her and embrace her in a hug. "Hey, you must be Gina. It's so good to meet you." I pull away and look at Will affectionately. "Will's been talking about you for ages."

She turns to him. "Is that right?"

"Oh yeah," I say and then lean toward her conspiratorially. "I even guessed you were the girl that had him all in a tizzy over a year ago."

Shock fills her face. "What?"

"Yeah, Will here was pretty pissy about a year or so ago, and I found out it was about a woman, but it was like pulling teeth to get any more information out of him. It wasn't until recently when I put two and two together and he caved and told me you were *her*."

She looks at Will, her expression still shocked, but there's also a softness to it, like she's coming to some kind of realization about him. Suddenly Rex barks and bounds toward another, much smaller dog. The owner's face morphs into terror as this giant pit bull runs straight toward her. Will must see it too because he curses and then chases after Rex.

I take the opportunity to talk to Gina without him around. I get only good vibes from her, and while I might be terrible when it comes to reading men, I'm a stellar judge of character when it comes to other women. I don't know why, maybe growing up with two very different sisters, but my gut has never been wrong when I meet a woman.

My gut tells me Gina's a good one, and I'm once again thankful that Will's finally so happy, but I also want to make sure she's not going to break his heart.

"So, Gina. What are your intentions with my brother?"

"What do you mean?"

"I mean, are you two just messing around, or is this serious?" I can already tell Will's serious about her.

"I'm pretty sure it's serious if we're meeting each other's families."

I look back over at Will who's currently reassuring a very nervous dog owner and nod at her response. "Good." I let out a small breath of relief that she and Will seem to be on the same page. The Edmonson sisters may be a hot mess right now, but at least one Edmonson is getting his shit together.

"I'm glad he finally let someone in."

"What do you mean?"

I watch my brother. "Will was really messed up after Candace died. I didn't think he'd ever get over it." I stop and look closely at Gina. "I'm grateful you're in his life. Maybe now he can put all those ghosts behind him."

Rex comes bounding back, and I immediately crouch down to meet him. I give him lots of love when he makes it to me and all the pain and heartache that's been exacerbated from Trent's silence eases in this moment.

My brother is happy, and I have a dog to take my mind off my life for a while.

We hang out at the park for the next few hours and then I invite myself over for dinner with them—mainly because the idea of being alone right now terrifies me. I feel like a china doll who was broken and put back together poorly, like one swift wind will break all my pieces all over again. Gina's quiet during dinner and then makes a quick exit afterward. Will's always been easy to read, probably because we're so close, both in age and in personalities. So I immediately worry when he seems distant and lost in his thoughts after Gina leaves.

"You okay?"

He glances at me. "Yeah, why?"

"You seem distracted."

He leans back in his chair and lets out a heavy sigh. "Gina seemed distant with me today, and I wanted to ask her about it, but *someone* had to invite herself to dinner."

I shrug, not feeling bad. He wouldn't either if he knew why I'm so hesitant to be alone. "I wanted to keep hanging out. This the first woman you've dated I actually liked."

"She's only the second woman I've dated."

"Exactly." I throw him a look because he knows what I'm talking about without me having to say it. Getting serious, I say, "Gina is really great, Will. I'm so glad you are finally letting someone in. I was worried about you."

"I know you were."

We talk a little more about our day together when Will switches gears. "So, how're things with you?"

Damn, I should've known this was coming.

"Ugh, can we not, please?"

"What? You can hassle me about my life, but I can't hassle you about yours?"

"Yep, pretty much." Plus, I can't talk about it with him. I can talk to Lainey and Elise because they don't know Trent that well. They were older or younger than us. But Will and I are only eleven months apart and had a lot of the same friends growing up, Trent included. He knows Trent. And he knows me. He'll be able to see through whatever lie I try to tell him, and I'm not ready to admit the truth, so it's better to not say anything.

He laughs. "Bullshit."

I shrug and take another drink of wine.

He watches me carefully and then says, "You're staying here tonight."

"That didn't sound like a question."

"It wasn't. If you think I'm going to let you drive home when you've been drinking, you clearly don't know who you're dealing with."

I blanche a little and put my glass down. It's only my third, but Will's been overly cautious about drinking and driving. And he has every right to be. After all, his fiancée died in a drunk-driving accident.

And frankly I don't want to fight him on this. I don't want to go back to my empty condo that's filled with memories of my night with Trent.

"Okay. I'll stay, but I'm stealing Rex. I need a cuddle buddy." I keep my voice light, but it's the truth. Rex may not be the warm body I wish was next to me in bed, but he'll do. And he won't break my heart, so that's a win in my book.

Will shakes his head. "I swear you're trying to steal my dog from me."

I rub my hands together. "You're on to my evil plan. Mwahaha."

"You're such a weirdo."

I can't help but genuinely smile at that. "Who do you think I learned it from?"

He rolls his eyes at me, and I am so thankful for my brother that I almost want to tell him about Trent.

And maybe someday I will.

24

TRENT

These have been the longest two weeks of my life. I thought eight months away from Becka was torture, but knowing I was so close to almost fixing things before I got pulled away again eats at me in a way touring didn't.

Tristan and I have been going nonstop since we landed in Texas to help our Aunt Jenny with Uncle Ted. Fortunately, his heart attack wasn't fatal. He's going to have to cut back big time on the bacon and other fatty foods he's grown used to being able to eat over the years, but he'll live. Since our small hometown of Bishop Ridge doesn't have a big hospital, we helped get him the best care in Austin and then stayed long enough to make sure that he was back on his feet, or at least in a position that wouldn't be a burden to our aunt. She's been hovering over him like a helicopter parent, and it's clear this rattled her foundation. My aunt and uncle have been together since they were teens and got married young. She's spent more of her life with him than without him. But this is the first time either of them has had a serious health issue, and it clearly hit her hard knowing how close she came to losing him.

It rattled Tris and me too. Our aunt and uncle are the only family we have left and have been more like parents to us than our real ones. I always found it fascinating that even though my mom and my aunt grew up in the same household, you couldn't find two people more different. While my aunt was always focused on school and getting good grades, my mom fell into the drug crowd.

My mom was twelve when she smoked her first joint. By fifteen, she was partying hard and experimenting with harder drugs. Then she met my dad when she was eighteen and started partying even harder. She apparently stopped doing drugs when she found out she was pregnant with me—at least that's what Aunt Jenny says. Since I didn't come out addicted to coke, I'm inclined to believe her. At least my mom did one thing right. She stayed sober until after Tristan was born. By then my parents had been together for a few years and were constantly fighting. My dad left, and that drove my mom to start drinking more. Then she found out that he overdosed and she spiraled. When cocaine didn't give her the high she wanted, she went deeper and tried heroin, and from there it was just a ticking time clock on her life. She lasted longer than we thought she would, but we spent several bouts living with our aunt and uncle while she claimed she was trying to get her life together again. I was eleven, Tristan nine, when my aunt and uncle finally got permanent custody, something they'd spent a long time fighting for. Our mom died two years later from an overdose.

When I got older, I begged my uncle to tell me the truth about my mom and what happened. I had been so young in the early years when my dad was around. When he told me my dad leaving was what finally broke her, all I could think was that she must've really loved him to throw her whole life away for a man who left her. To throw away her kids. I'll never forget that she chose drugs over us. I've worked hard to forgive her, and I have—mostly. But I'll never forget.

Being back here in Texas, it's not my mom I can't stop thinking about. It's all the memories that came after. My uncle seeing how listless Tristan and I were. Him teaching us how to play guitar and piano. The first time I wrote my feelings down as a song and Tristan and I wrote music for it. Playing with Will and Becka in the neighborhood, riding bikes, playing flag football on the muddy grass after a big storm, meeting Kasen and Miles in my first band class in high school, forming the band, my first kiss—with Becka no less.

All those memories pummel me the entire time I'm here. It's been a long time since we've spent this much time in Texas, and even though I love getting to spend time with my aunt and uncle, I'm more than ready to get back to LA by the time they drop us off at the airport.

When the plane lands at LAX, I turn to Tristan. "I'm getting a separate ride from you. I'm going to Becka's."

The corner of his lips lift in response and he just nods. He doesn't fight me on it or tell me I'm insane to still be chasing this woman after she's basically blown me off for eight months.

But I can't give her up. Not until she tells me to my face that she doesn't want me.

I'm tired of her pushing me away, and I can't stand the distance between us anymore. I miss her, and I need her as much as I need my next breath.

This time I'm going to fight for what I really want.

I should've known she wouldn't be home when I showed up. I pace in front of her door for a minute thinking about what my next step should be when her car pulls up and parks. She gets out of the car and rubs her eyes before locking it and starting to make her way to her front door. And a horrible thought runs through my head. Did she not sleep here last night?

Am I too late?

My heart drops to my stomach faster than a brick in water, but

I hold myself together because this feels like my last shot, and even if I'm too late, at least she'll know where I stand.

Her foot hits the sidewalk before she looks up and sees me standing at her front door. She stops immediately, and her lips part slightly before her entire posture changes and becomes more guarded. Her shoulders are stiffer and higher than when she's relaxed, her arms crossed in front of her.

Her body language screams closed off, but her eyes say something else. There's a look there that I can feel in my own gaze—longing. Like the thing you want most in the world is standing right in front of you.

It's been so long since I last laid eyes on her, and I feel every minute that's kept us apart like it's a visceral thing. Fuck, I've missed her.

Her expression goes neutral and then she's walking toward me, and I can barely breathe with how badly I want to kiss her. She walks past me and sticks the key in the door, and for a minute I think she's actually going to walk into her condo and leave me out here without saying a word to me.

I hear the lock turn and then she grabs the handle, but she doesn't open the door, nor does she turn around. "What are you doing here?"

There's no anger in her voice, but she's not exactly welcoming me either.

"I thought we needed to talk."

She opens the door and walks in, then turns around and stands there with the door wide open for me to follow her through. I don't hesitate. I walk into her apartment and am immediately thrown back to that night.

To the taste of her on my tongue, her cries of pleasure, the feel of her pussy squeezing me so tight.

I close my eyes and soak in the memories until I can feel her standing behind my back clearly waiting for me to say whatever I came here to say. I can see I'm going to have to initiate.

But she surprises me. "That night," she starts, and I turn

around, my gaze intently focused on her. "...it wasn't a mistake to me."

Those words are fucking music to my ears, but it's also a painful reminder that in my attempt to be noble and not fuck up our friendship, I actually ruined what could've been an amazing relationship this whole damn time. Because standing here staring at her now after an eight-month tour, I'm surer than I've ever been about anything in my life that Becka is it for me.

She's everything. My friend. My lover. My whole fucking world.

She looks at me, indignation on her face like she's ready for me to fight her on whatever she's about to say. "I can't be friends with you, Trent."

I step toward her and don't hesitate to grab her behind the neck and bring her mouth up to mine until our lips are only a breath apart. She inhales sharply, and her hands grab my biceps to brace herself.

"Good, because I don't want to be your fucking friend."

And then I kiss her.

I kiss her with eight months' worth of pent-up need, desire, heartache. I put it all in my kiss, and with every touch of our lips, our tongues, I feel her give it all back to me. She moans low in her throat and then slides her hands around my waist while my hand buries itself deep in her hair. I hold her to me, my tongue sliding across hers and making love to her mouth the way I want to make love to her body.

Desire blooms fierce in my belly and with a growl, I move my hands to grip under her ass and lift her up. Her legs automatically go around my hips, and I continue to kiss her as I carry her through her condo to her bedroom. I place her next to the bed but still can't force myself to break away from our kiss.

Fuck, her mouth is heaven.

I feel her long, delicate fingers reach for my belt buckle and quickly strip it off me. She pulls away and when I open my eyes, hers are liquid fire. Her lips are red and swollen from our kiss, and she's panting as much as I am. Then her lips quirk up in a seductive grin at the same time that she unzips my pants and grips my cock over my boxer briefs.

I close my eyes and tilt my head back, fighting back a groan. God, it's been so long since she's touched me—since anyone has. My hand and memories of my one night with Becka have been the only company I had all tour, and I'm feeling it now as my balls tighten, my cock thickens, and my breath catches in my chest.

I don't know if I'm going to last long.

"Becka..." Her name is a prayer from my lips. I'm torn between wanting her to stop so I can come inside her and wanting her to never stop because just having her touch me again feels like the greatest fucking gift I've ever been given.

"I've imagined this so many times," she says so softly I almost don't hear her.

I look down in time to see her push my pants and underwear off and then without any hesitation, she drops to her knees, swipes her tongue across the tip of my cock, and I'm lost to her. She licks me like she's been on a diet and she's finally getting to have some ice cream. Any attempts to fight my body's response disappear and I groan loudly, but I can no longer look away. It's a struggle to keep my eyes open because it feels so fucking good, but I also want to memorize every movement, every swipe of her tongue, how her cheeks hollow when she sucks on me, how her gorgeous lips part wide when she attempts to take me in farther.

When I hit the back of her throat, I come undone. I slide my fingers through her hair and guide her head as she bobs up and down on my cock. Her eyes heat and she lets out a moan that tells me she likes what I'm doing, so I don't stop.

"Fuck, I'm gonna come."

I watch mesmerized as her eyes light up and the edges of her mouth tip up slightly in what I know would be a smile if her mouth wasn't otherwise occupied. Determination fills her gaze and then she goes down on me with so much gusto I'm left breathless. I hit the back of her throat again, but this time instead of immediately bobbing back up, she holds me there and swallows.

And I come so hard I see stars.

My eyes close on their own accord, the bliss too much as I release down her throat, and I swear nothing has ever been sexier than when she pulls off and gives my tip another lick and wipes her mouth.

I shudder from her touch, my tip overly sensitive after my much-needed release, and then collapse on the bed.

"Come here," I say, my breath still coming out in hard pants.

She lies down next to me, and I wrap my arm around her, pulling her close until she's resting her head on my shoulder and her body is snuggled up next to mine.

"Give me five minutes and then I'll be ready for round two."

She rubs her hand along my stomach, and as it turns out, I don't need five minutes after all.

25

Becka

My face is smooshed against a warm body, and for a second I don't want to wake up. I don't want this to be a dream. I inhale deeply, soaking in Trent's manly scent. I don't know if it's a cologne he wears or his deodorant, but he always smells so fucking good.

He's still passed out, and I can't blame him. We had more sex last night than I've ever had in a twenty-four-hour period. With a long look at him, I gently move off the bed, grab my robe, and then tiptoe from the room, closing the door softly behind me. I lean back against the door, trying to wrap my head around everything.

I thought I would feel different if Trent and I got together.

Are we even together? Or is he going to tell me he wants a friends with benefits situation? Am I setting myself up for heartbreak all over again?

My stomach clenches, and I fight back the bile that rises in my throat. I'm used to guys pulling the rug out from under me, but the idea of Trent doing it hurts more than ever.

Needing a distraction, I look around my apartment and decide it could use a good deep clean. I grab my cleaning supplies, put on my gloves, and get to work doing anything I can to keep myself from thinking about what happens when Trent wakes up. I dust my living room, dining room, and kitchen. I fluff up the pillows on my couch. I deep clean the bathroom. Then I move to the kitchen, sweeping and mopping the floor before I decide to clean and reorganize my fridge.

I'm on my knees, my upper half inside my fridge while I scrub at a spot where a condiment of some kind must've spilled when I hear Trent's voice behind me.

"It's seven in the morning. What the hell are you doing?"

I sit up and glance at him, trying to see if his expression will give away how he's feeling about us. He just looks at me with amused curiosity which doesn't tell me much of anything except that he probably thinks I'm a little crazy.

"I'm cleaning."

He arches a brow and can no longer fight back his grin. "I see that. Is this something you normally do this early in the morning?"

"Um, not usually, no."

He tilts his head, his eyes intense as his grin slowly fades. "What's going on?"

Instinctually, I want to say nothing, but I've avoided talking to Trent for eight months and it didn't get us anywhere. "I, um...I clean when I'm anxious. I wasn't quite sure what to expect, you know, when you woke up. Last time...well, last time wasn't exactly what I had expected and—"

Understanding dawns on his face. "And you thought I'd say I want to be just friends again."

It's hard to hold his gaze when I'm feeling so vulnerable, but I do. "Something like that."

He nods, and I can practically see the wheels in his head turning. "Well, we'll just have to wipe that horrible morning from your memory, won't we? I say we replace it with orgasms."

I let out a startled laugh. "What?"

One side of his mouth lifts in a charismatic smile that I would totally expect of a rock star. "You heard me. Orgasms. Lots and lots of orgasms. Starting now." He kneels down on the floor and guides me until I'm lying on my back, and I'm grateful I already swept and mopped this floor.

"What are you doing?"

His eyes gleam. "Eating breakfast."

And then he leans down, opens my robe, and makes me forget anything exists but him.

I'm deliciously sore when I make my way into work the next day. Normally Mondays feel like they drag forever, but the day passes quickly. I head to my last meeting of the day, and instead of dreading it like I had been when I saw it on my calendar on Friday, I'm now excited to talk about the Rapturous Intent documentary.

"So, Fletcher says that editing is on track and they should have the preview ready for us next week. From there, execs will decide if anything needs to be changed, or if it's good as is," Simone says.

"Is there concern it'll need another round of edits after the preview?" I ask.

She gets a conspiratorial smile on her face, "Well, Becka, they are rock stars after all. I'm sure the camera caught some things that weren't exactly aboveboard. You can't have rock 'n' roll without the sex and drugs."

She turns to the rest of the group and continues while I sit back in my chair and process her words. "Of course, since we're a subscription service, we have a lot more wiggle room to show sex and drugs. We just need to make sure it's classy, and if it crosses the line, we'll cut it. We don't want to ruin these guys or no other celebs will ever want to work with us."

Everyone nods in agreement, and the energy in the room has

definitely gone up. We're all eager to see how it turned out, but my excitement has dimmed in the aftermath of Simone's words.

Am I going to have to watch Trent with other women?

We never talked about what happened on tour. We were a little busy doing *other* things. It didn't even cross my mind to ask how many women he'd been with in the past eight months. My stomach swirls with nausea at the idea. But what right do I even have to be mad? I'm the one who ignored him. Of course, he'd hook up with other women. He was single.

But still, I feel a little heartbroken because I couldn't even think about having sex with someone else in all the time we were apart.

By the end of the meeting, I'm relieved that it's my last one of the day because my head is a mess, and all I want to do is talk to Trent. We already have plans, and he should be at my place by the time I get there. The whole drive home I keep going back and forth on whether or not I want to know.

When I pull up and see his handsome face break out into a huge smile at my arrival, I decide I don't want to know. What good will it do? None. It'll just add to my long list of insecurities, and I don't need any help in that department.

He greets me with a passionate kiss that leaves my panties wet and my heart beating rapidly in my chest. I don't know how he does it, but just being in his arms soothes me. I lean my head against his chest, wrap my arms around his waist, and hold him tight. I need to let this go and move forward with him. The past doesn't matter.

"You okay?" He murmurs against my hair, his arms wrapped around me.

"Long day."

"You sure that's it?"

I pull away just enough to look up at him and see in his eyes his concern for me. "How'd you know something was bothering me?"

He smiles his cocky grin, and I'd roll my eyes if I wasn't so curious. "I know you, Becka. Obviously more than you realize. So, you gonna tell me what's up?"

"It's nothing. We were just talking about the documentary today at work, and it made me think about our time apart...and you on tour..."

He squints, waiting for more, but I remain silent. "Uh-huh. Go on."

I shrug my shoulders, and then finally roll my eyes because I feel ridiculous that I'm letting this eat at me so much. "And how many women were constantly around you."

His piercing gaze never leaves my face, and I wish I knew what he seems so intent on finding in my gaze. He finally brushes a stray lock of hair from my face and tucks it behind my ear. He lets his hand rest there cupping my jaw and making sure I'm still looking at him. I feel immensely vulnerable right now, like he can see into my soul, but I don't dare look away. I'm too mesmerized by his ocean-blue eyes.

"I was on the road for months without you, thinking nothing could happen with you. You want to know how many women I slept with?"

A surge of adrenaline blooms in my chest, and my heart constricts painfully as emotion clogs my throat. Is he trying to punish me for all the months I gave him silence by making me hear this? "How could you possibly think I'd want to know that?"

I step away from him, but he grabs my upper arms and holds me close, not painfully, but securely so that I'm still forced to look at him. "None."

My breath freezes in my lungs, my heart stops, and the silence that follows that one word makes me question if I heard him right. "What?"

"None, Becka. Not a one. I didn't even consider it. All I could think about was you. None of those women came close to tempting me because none of them were you." He brushes his thumb across the apple of my cheek. "You're the only one I want. I know you're worried I'll be tempted or leave you, but you're stuck with me now because I'm hooked. I already gave you up once, and it was torture. I can't do it again, Becka. I need you."

I want to believe him more than I want my next breath.

I don't want to be this girl who lets her daddy issues ruin the best thing she's ever had—a friend and a lover all wrapped in one. A man who's seen me at all the various stages of my life and never judged me. A man who after eight months of silence still returned to me, his heart in his hands.

The truth is I need him too.

I need him to prove to me that there are good guys out there. I need him to help me believe that I'm enough. I need *him*. Simple as that.

I tuck my insecurities away, knowing I'll need to work harder at getting them under control with my therapist, but not wanting them to ruin anything more tonight.

And I choose to believe him.

26

TRENT

The cashier hands me a plastic bag with my purchase inside with shaky hands, her eyes still wide and a giddy smile on her face. I throw her a grin, slide my sunglasses on, and walk out of the store already knowing she's going to be bragging to all her friends that she sold Trent Bridger a sex toy.

It comes with the territory, although I can't say I've ever bought a sex toy for a partner before. But Becka is having doubts. I've known her a long time, which means I can read her better than her past boyfriends, even if we've only been together officially for a week.

I need Becka to trust me in a way she's never trusted anyone else. I need her unrestrained passion, her soft open eyes. I need her to believe me when I say I'm not going anywhere, not mentally or emotionally anyway. I'll have to go on tour again after we release our next album, which we're already working on. But that doesn't mean I'm going to abandon her.

I don't know if it's our years of friendship that came before our first kiss, or the years of friendship after that have led to her quickly owning my heart. One week with her and I'm already addicted. Her laugh, her ridiculously corny jokes, even the way she gets completely irrational when she's hungry—all of it endears her to me even more.

But I think it's the way she looks at me that's really enthralled me. When she looks at me, she doesn't see the rock star. Her eyes don't get that starry-eyed, can't-believe-I'm-standing-before-someone-famous look. No, when Becka looks at me, her jade-green eyes get soft, and the corners of her lips lift in the gentlest of smiles. My heart pounds furiously in my chest, and determination fills my soul with the knowledge that I can't lose this woman.

But she's still cautious. There's still a part of her that she's holding back, and I know today's lesson—for lack of a better word—won't totally wipe that away, but I'm hoping it's a step in the right direction.

I knock on her front door, feeling an unhealthy mix of eagerness and terror. There's a very real possibility she could attempt to castrate me for this idea. But I'm willing to risk it because if she says yes, the reward will be worth it.

Oh so worth it.

She opens the door, and instantly her face lights up. My heart drums in my chest, and I swear I'm going to memorize the rhythm and turn it into a song just for her.

"Hey, this is a nice surprise," she says.

"I had an idea."

Becka quirks her head and gets an amused expression on her face. "Did it hurt?"

God, she's such a smart-ass sometimes. I fucking love it. "Hardy har har. Let me in and I'll tell you what my brilliant idea was." At least, I hope she thinks it's brilliant.

She opens her door wider, but only moves aside slightly, so I have to press my body against hers on my way inside. I can't resist leaning down, gently pushing her against the wall, and kissing her hard until we're both breathless. Then I walk to her living room, discreetly adjusting myself while pretending that I'm not ridiculously affected by her presence.

"So, what was this idea you had?" she asks, her voice still noticeably breathless from our kiss.

"I was thinking of having a field trip, but with a surprise element." I open the bag I brought with me and pull out the package, holding it up to her.

"What's that?" she asks as she reaches out and takes it from my hands.

"Consider this a trust exercise, but with a sexy twist."

Her jaw drops and her gaze snaps up to mine as soon as she realizes what it is. "A vibrator!"

I nod and pull out the remote that I removed from the package after I bought it. "You wear it, but I control it."

She looks a little breathless, and for a minute I wonder if she really will kill me for this, but then she looks back down at the box and begins opening it up. She pulls out the small bullet shaped vibrator that's about as long as her pointer finger, but about as thick as two fingers. She looks back at me and then back at the vibe, and I can tell she's considering it. I feel a little giddy that she hasn't shut me down completely.

"Wait, you said something about a field trip."

"Oh, yeah. I have a band thing at Amoeba. We're doing a small interview and then a live performance. You're coming with me, and we're going to take this bad boy for a test drive."

Her gorgeous eyes go wide again, and I watch her throat move as she swallows nervously. When she speaks, I'm not surprised that her voice comes out a little breathy, and I can't lie—it makes me hard.

"You want me to wear this in public?"

"Yup."

"And you're going to turn it on? While we're in public?"

I smile wide, and I probably look like the Grinch when he was plundering Whoville, but I feel like I'm about to plunder a village of my own—Beckaville.

Fuck, that's cheesy, but it still thrills me.

I nod again, because if I speak now, she'll know how fucking eager I am to do this—if she can't tell by my face alone and the fact that I'm pretty sure I'm practically bouncing on my feet at the idea.

She nibbles her lip. "A trust exercise?"

"Mmhmm."

Determination fills her gaze, and I know before she even says the words that she's on board. "Okay. Are we doing this now?"

I fight back my pleasure at her acquiescence. "Yes ma'am, we are. Go put that in, and we'll head out."

She spins on her heels and goes to the bathroom. She comes out five minutes later, her cheeks already flushed. "I can't believe I'm doing this," she mumbles as she grabs her purse and then locks up after we get outside.

I take her hand in mine and kiss the crown of her head. "Thank you for trusting me enough to do this."

Her eyes are filled with worry for the briefest moment. "You won't make me look ridiculous, right? Or embarrass me?"

I shake my head, my expression turning serious. "Never, Becks." I brush my thumb across her cheek and down her jaw, unable to keep from touching her. "I would never do that to you, but I want to pleasure you. Always. And while this thing comes with a remote, it also can be controlled from an app on my phone which means I can pleasure you even when I have to be away from you."

Her eyes get that soft, tender look again, and my heart speeds up. God, I love when she looks at me like this. She gets up on her tiptoes and kisses me, the tenderness from her gaze matching the tenderness in her kiss, and I soak it all up.

I spend the drive to Amoeba Music in Hollywood holding her hand and giving her heated glances every chance I get. It's impossible not to be turned on at the idea that I have control over her pleasure for the foreseeable future. At a red light, I decide to give it a little test drive. I discreetly reach my left hand into my pocket and press the top button which I know turns it on, as well as increases the power.

Becka inhales sharply and then squeezes my hand. I glance over and see her staring at me, her eyes dark and needy, her lips parted, and her breasts jiggling slightly with every panted breath.

Okay, so I might've hit the button more than once.

She squeezes my hand tighter and then drops her head back against the seat and lets out a groan. "Oh my God."

My pants suddenly feel unbelievably tight, and I'm questioning whether or not *I* can do this without taking her somewhere private, ripping that vibrator from her body, and slamming my already steel-hard cock inside her.

A car horn beeps angrily behind me, and I face forward to see that the light is green. Shit. I press the gas but can barely concentrate with Becka writhing in the seat next to me. Needing to save my sanity and make sure we get to the venue safely, I turn the vibe off.

Becka lets out a sigh, and I glance over just long enough to notice her legs slightly shaking while she rubs her hands up and down her thighs like she's trying to dispel some of the pleasure.

"Please tell me that was the highest setting, or I'm definitely going to embarrass myself."

It wasn't. It was probably only the third setting out of ten possible options. This is definitely going to get interesting.

The rest of the drive is uneventful, and once I get parked I'm swept up in all the band obligations. Amoeba Music is a record store in Hollywood that has made a historic name for itself in the music industry. It's always reminded me of the store in the film *Empire Records*, but it's more famous. I'm excited to play here because they always have a pulse on what music is up and coming.

The interview starts, and the host, Janie, asks me most of the questions. I keep my left hand in my pocket, maintaining a casual lounge pose. I'm just waiting for the minute she finally asks a question to someone else, so I can discreetly watch Becka, who's standing with Robbie near the wall closest to me and tucked behind most of the fans that have come out to see us perform.

Finally, I get my chance when Janie asks a question to the whole band and Miles takes the opportunity to answer.

I press the top button again and immediately watch Becka's eyes widen before they close slowly in bliss. Even from my seat on this small, raised platform, I can see her trying to control her body—and failing miserably. Robbie glances over at her and she looks up, her gaze connecting with mine even as I see her mouth move to answer whatever he's asked her.

I press the button again and can see her body tense. Her cheeks pink up and she bites her lip, but her gaze never leaves mine, and it's almost like she's challenging me to give her more.

She's fucking sexy as sin like this, her gaze heated and determined. I press the button again and then have to cross my ankle over my knee to hide the effect she's having on my body.

I should be focusing on the interview; I know I should. But she's so tempting and she makes me want to be a little reckless, which is very much not like me. I'm the papa bear who keeps things running—well, me and Robbie. But here I am acting like a foolish youth seeing how much I can get away with before I'm caught.

And she's right here with me.

The trust she's bestowing in me slams into me and nearly knocks all the breath from my lungs. I must show some kind of shock because Tristan leans over and whispers, "You okay?"

"Yep," I say, but it sounds hoarse, probably because I'm having trouble breathing right now as I watch Becka. I have a perfect view of her from my position. I can see her hands clenched at her sides and her legs crossed in a weak attempt to diminish the pleasure.

No way, baby girl. Not today. Today you'll feel it all.

Fuck, I can't wait to be inside her.

The host wraps up the interview and gives us five minutes to take a break before we need to set up for the performance portion. I immediately ditch the guys and head straight for Becka. Robbie meets me halfway—no doubt going to check the setup because he's just that great—and stops me, saying, "I think Becka might be sick. She seems a little flushed and uncomfortable."

I fight back a laugh. I'll bet she is. I pat him on the back. "Thanks, man. I'm going to take care of it right now."

I don't wait to see his reaction. I reach Becka, grab her hand, and drag her to the back of the store, finding the employee bathroom. I guide her inside, then close and lock the door. She immediately pounces on me the second I turn around.

"You better turn this thing off or turn it the fuck up because I need to come desperately," she says in between kisses.

I grab the back of her neck and hold her to my mouth, plundering hers with my tongue. She moans deliciously and grinds her body against mine as she straddles my leg. In this position, I can faintly hear the vibe, but I can definitely feel it as she grinds against me seeking release.

Deciding she's—okay, *we've*—suffered enough, I unbutton her pants and slide my hand inside her panties, growling at how slick she is, and then start rubbing her clit until she's coming, her chest heaving with breathy pants and sweat glistening at the edge of her hairline. She comes a second time almost right on top of the first before I grab the remote from my pocket with my free hand and turn off the vibe.

She immediately sags against me, her body limp and tired, while my cock is harder than it's ever been. I kiss her dewy forehead. "Have I told you lately how sexy you are?"

"No," she says, still trying to catch her breath. "But feel free to start any time."

I bark out a laugh and then hug her close. I love having her here with me, and I love the fact that she was willing to be this adventurous with me. I know it's out of her comfort zone, and her trust means everything.

She pulls away and looks up at me, her eyes shining with contentment that I suspect matches mine. "What about you?"

"I'll be fine until we get to my place after this and I can ravage you properly."

"You sure? I could give you a bathroom blowjob. I've never done that before either." I have to smile at her willingness, but I don't want her this way in some dirty bathroom. I want her on a bed where I can take all the time in the world giving her more pleasure than she knows what to do with.

"I won't turn down a blowjob later, but this was all I wanted." I brush her hair away from her face and run my fingers through the brown strands.

"Trent?"

"Yeah?"

Her eyes are shining, and her lips are tilted up in a smile. "Thank you."

She doesn't have to say it, but I know she's not just thanking me for the orgasms. She's thanking me for pushing her, for knowing her, for wanting her.

Truth is I think I've always wanted her. Now I'm just making up for lost time.

27

BECKA

Something's going on with Will.

He's avoiding my calls, and I'm desperate to tell him about Trent. I thought eight months of keeping Trent a secret was hard, but after spending two weeks with him and rarely spending any time apart, I'm dying to finally tell my brother.

Everything with Trent feels different than it has with other guys. We spend every night together, making dinner together, watching TV together, having leg-shaking sex together. It feels perfect. I don't know if I've ever been this happy.

Which also scares me, but I'm trying not to sabotage this. I know it's my insecurities that are making me feel scared, and I refuse to let them ruin what finally feels like a solid and healthy relationship. I've continued to see my therapist, and while things still feel like they're improving at a snail's pace, they are, in fact, improving. I'll take progress, no matter how small.

But part of that progress also means I need to finally admit to my family that Trent and I are a thing, and I feel like I need to tell Will first, especially given how close we all were growing up. I don't want him to feel weird about this or disapprove of my relationship. But I can't tell him if he doesn't answer his fucking phone.

So I decide to go to his house. If he won't answer his phone, then he's going to have to see me face-to-face. And he can't keep me out of his house since I have the spare key. Trent wanted to come—because he feels like we're in this together and should talk to Will at the same time—but he got pulled away for an emergency band meeting, and I didn't want to wait any longer. I feel like I've waited too long as it is.

I knock, but when he doesn't answer, I use my spare key and am immediately overwhelmed by the stench in his living room. Rex comes running over to me, his tongue lolling out of his mouth, and I look around Will's living room in absolute shock. There are beer cans everywhere, takeout boxes, and a lump on the couch that I slowly realize is my brother.

"Will?" I rush over, suddenly terrified that someone died and he didn't tell me. "Will!" I shout, shaking his shoulder.

He grumbles and then squints one eye open. "Becka?" His voice is still drowsy with sleep, and when he sits up, I have to step back because someone desperately needs a shower.

"What the hell is going on?" I ask.

He looks at me like he's not sure if I'm really standing in his living room or if I'm a figment of his imagination. "Will? Seriously, what is all this?" I ask, gesturing to the disaster that is his house. It looks like he invited every frat house in SoCal to come hang out in his living room, and it smells worse than the boys' locker room used to smell when we were in high school.

He rubs his eyes with the heel of his palm and then rests his elbows on his knees, and his whole body sags with what can only be described as defeat. "Gina and I broke up."

My face goes slack in complete and utter shock. That is the last thing I expected. They were happy and in love when I saw them only a few weeks ago. "What happened?"

He shakes his head, and alarm bells start going off in my brain. I sit down on his couch—brushing off crumbs and an empty beer can first—and then place a hand on his arm. "Will, tell me what happened. You both seemed so happy."

He turns his head, and instantly his eyes flash with anger, but it's gone so fast I almost wonder if I imagine it, especially when he sounds so broken when he says, "She deserves better."

"Better than you? Did she say why she broke up with you?"

He frowns at me. "I broke up with her."

I slap his arm. "What the fuck, Will!"

"What?"

"Why would you do that? She was perfect for you!"

"Beat a guy while he's down, why don't ya." He's trying to joke with me, but his lips barely quirk into a semblance of a smile, and his eyes remain vacant and lost.

"You need to fix this." I immediately start thinking of all the things he could do to get her back.

"No, I don't. She's better off." There's something in his voice that makes me pause. He believes that.

This might be the first moment I see my brother as the broken little boy he was when my dad left. Will stepped up after that, and he's always been put-together. Or at least more together than the rest of us. Even Lainey, who can be very type A, is clearly a hot mess underneath all her perfection.

But Will always seemed steady and sure. It wasn't until Candace—and her subsequent death—that he seemed to change. But even then I never saw him as low as he is now. Maybe it's not just the Edmonson girls that let their insecurities ruin their relationships.

Maybe all of us Edmonson kids are messed up adults. We have jobs and function in society, but there's something broken internally.

"Will, I don't want to have to torture it out of you. You know I am a pro at giving wet willies, even to a pro football player. So is it going to be little sister torture, or will you give me the truth freely? Either way, I'm gonna find out what happened."

He glances at me, his stare gauging how serious I am and then finally heaves the heaviest, most dramatic sigh I've ever heard from my fairly stoic brother. "I fell in love with her."

"Heaven forbid."

He glares at me. "There are things you don't know, Becks. Things about me. I'm a mess, okay? Is that what you want to know? She deserves someone better."

I ignore the comment about me not knowing things about him—clearly I'm not the only one keeping secrets—and focus on what's important. "But she wanted you."

He opens his mouth to refute my comment, but then closes it and stares at nothing.

"Will, are you still seeing your therapist?" Will finally caved and started seeing a therapist a while back, but I haven't heard him talk about it in a long time, and since he seemed like he was doing so well, I didn't bother to ask. But he's clearly spiraling if the state of his living room is any indication.

He needs help. More than I can give him.

"Why does everyone ask me that?" he mumbles, and I have to wonder who else he's been talking to. "No, I stopped my therapy sessions a while ago."

"Maybe it'd be worth starting them back up again. You look miserable and heartbroken. I hate seeing you this way."

And because he's so miserable, I bite back the words that were clawing at my throat the whole way here. I don't tell him that I'm dating Trent, or that I'm quite possibly completely in love with him. How can I share my happiness with my brother when he looks so sad? It feels like bragging that you won the lottery to a homeless person.

Will rubs his face again, and when he looks back up at me, his eyes are shining. My big, masculine, stoic brother is on the verge of tears, and my chest aches from the pain I see in his eyes.

"I messed it all up," he whispers, further breaking my heart.

I reach out, put a hand on his arm, and say, "It's never too late to fix it."

Instead of giving him hope like I'd been going for, his eyes look haunted. "Sometimes it is."

I stay with my brother for the rest of the day, much to his

dismay. He clearly wants to be alone, but I'm not about to abandon him when he's going through hell. That's not what we do. We've always had each other's backs—at least when we've been honest about what's going on in our lives. As the day goes on, I can't stop thinking about what Will hasn't told me. It's obviously something big and something he's still not willing to share. It makes me wonder all the more about what my brother's been hiding from me and for how long.

When I finally get in my car to go home, I think about all the months I kept Trent a secret and worry that maybe my brother and I aren't as close as we always thought.

28

TRENT

Getting a call about an emergency band meeting to hold a last-minute intervention with Kasen was not on my agenda for today. We've all known for a while that his substance abuse had started back up, but lately he's become erratic and unreliable, and we can't afford that when we're about to head into the studio to record our new album.

Kasen paces back and forth in front of us, his hands gripping his hair in frustration and his usually carefree grin nowhere to be found. "I'm fine, guys. I have everything under control."

"Bullshit," Miles spits out, and I'm surprised by the anger in his voice. Miles is our chill one. Not the guy who gets pissed off. But he's been a lot more sensitive about drugs and Kasen's repeated fall-down-the-hole behavior since his brother sold us out for drug money.

Kasen stops his pacing, and I notice his hands shaking at his sides. His eyes are a little wild, and I wonder how long it's been since he last used.

"I saw you with Charli," Miles says, and my gaze darts to him. This is news to me, but a glance at Tristan tells me he knew about it. "I've had my suspicions for a while since she started showing up at the same parties we were always at, but then I finally saw you two together."

Kasen immediately shakes his head. "That was nothing. Just two old friends."

"Some friend to leave you for dead," Tristan mumbles, his face a moody glower.

Kasen throws him a glare and then turns back to Miles. "I'm serious, dude. It's all good. I'm fine."

Even as he says the words, sweat glistens along his hairline, and he can't stop moving.

"What was it this time?" I ask, cutting to the chase. I'm sick of this denial bullshit. I'm supposed to be with Becka telling Will about us right now and instead Kasen is wasting our time with lies when we can all tell he's using again, and not just weed. His body shows all the signs that we've become too familiar with over our years in this life.

Kasen looks at me, but he can't hold my gaze. Whether because it's been too long since he had a hit or because he's feeling guilty as fuck, I'm not sure.

"Kase. We love you, but you need to tell us what drugs you're doing. Is it just coke again? Or is it something else?" Robbie asks, his voice calm and soothing instead of its usual happy and joking tone.

Kase rubs his hands through his hair again, and for a minute I think he's going to throw out another denial, but then he surprises me. He scrubs his face and then sits heavily on the couch as if his body suddenly weighs too much for him to hold it up. He doesn't look at us when he confesses. "Mostly coke."

Mostly. That's the word I hear the loudest, meaning there's more. "What else?" I ask, my gaze immediately going to his arms looking for track marks.

He shakes his head, and when he looks up at us, he looks so lost and broken that my gut clenches. "I'll go back to rehab."

Tristan frowns at him. "Why won't you tell us?"

Kasen just shakes his head. Tristan and I glance at each other, our expressions matching with worry. Robbie goes over to the couch and sits next to him.

"Kase. You can tell us. You know we always have your back. We're worried about you."

Kasen's eyes water like he's on the verge of tears, and his gaze fills with shame. "Heroin."

He says it so softly I'm convinced I heard him wrong. Robbie's face goes white, and I look around at each of the guys, all of us coming to the same realization at the same time.

This is way worse than last time.

Kasen is going to need a lot more help than any of us can give him. This goes way beyond the buddy system and trying to watch him whenever we go to parties. He needs rehab and a professional who can help him kick this for good.

"And Charli?" Miles asks, his gaze focused intently on Kasen, his voice low and deeper than I think I've ever heard it.

Kasen's shoulders sag. "We're not dating. She's my dealer."

Miles stands so fast, his chair tips over. Without a word, he grabs his coat and storms out of my house. Tristan, Robbie, and I all exchange a glance, clearly worried about him, but Kasen needs us more right now. He's falling apart, tears now streaming down his face and his hands shaking in his lap.

"I can kick it on my own. It's not that bad yet. I only used it a couple of times."

"You just said you'd go to rehab," Robbie gently reminds him, and I've never been so grateful for him because I'm struggling to be the leader right now. Looking at Kasen is reminding me too much of my mom's breakdowns when she swore she was done and would get clean. She did, but only for short bouts of time. It never lasted, and I don't think it'll last with Kasen either. There are too many temptations in our world for him to do this on his own.

Kasen shakes his head, like I suspected he would. He didn't really mean it when he said he'd go to rehab. He said it because he knew that's what we wanted to hear.

He's a drug addict in the throes of it. And if there's anything my mom taught me it's that addicts lie, even to the ones they love.

The hours pass, and Miles doesn't return. Kasen continues to go back and forth between agreeing to rehab and saying he can do it on his own. Robbie, whose heart is bigger than his brain, offers to help him through his withdrawals and make sure he gets back on his feet. He doesn't realize that's a futile attempt. Kasen is beyond our simple help. He needs more. He needs a professional. But arguing won't change things. Kasen needs to want help or else it'll be a waste of time, just like his last round of rehab.

Tristan is quiet through most of this, which isn't exactly surprising—my brother isn't a big talker—but I still worry about him. He was old enough to remember Mom when she was like this, and if it's affecting me, I'm sure it's affecting him. He helps Kasen into Robbie's car and then leaves with just a simple hug. I don't know where he's going, and I don't ask. I probably should, but Tris deals with things in his own way, usually between the legs of a willing woman or writing a song that will end up breaking all our hearts and being a chart-topping hit.

I collapse on my couch, feeling like the weight of the whole damn world is on my chest. I check the time on my phone and make a snap decision to go to Becka's. It's late, but not too late. She should still be up. I send her a text to make sure. I'm not going to be great company, but I need her. I need her soothing voice and hands. I need her warmth so I don't feel so lost and helpless like I do sitting in my big house all by myself.

Becka responds almost immediately telling me to come over. She doesn't have to tell me twice. I'm in my car and heading to her place without a second thought.

She opens the door and immediately opens her arms inviting me in for a hug. I wrap her in my arms and hold her tight against me feeling all my worries ease while I hold her close. I'm not sure how long we stand there in our embrace, but she doesn't rush me. Her small hands slide up and down my back in soothing motions, and my shoulders eventually drop from their tense position by my ears.

When we finally break from our hug, she pulls me inside her condo. "Want anything to drink?"

I shake my head. "I just want to hold you."

Her smile is soft as she climbs onto the couch and cuddles up next to me. We lie there together, not talking, just touching. I slide my fingers through her silky brown hair, feeling immensely grateful that I was able to fix things between us because this is exactly what I needed.

Eventually I break the silence. "How'd it go with Will?" She tenses slightly in my arms, and my body tightens up bracing for more bad news.

"I couldn't tell him," she whispers. She tilts her head where it's resting on my chest so that she can look me in the eyes. "He broke up with Gina." That takes me by surprise. They seemed so happy at our concert.

"He was a mess when I got there. I've never seen him like that, and I couldn't tell him our happy news when he's so miserable."

I want to believe her, but a part of me is worried she's not telling him because she doesn't think this will last. Maybe I'm just feeling exceptionally raw after the day I've had, but urgency spreads through me. Am I the only one who's one hundred percent invested in us?

"Where do you see our relationship going?" I ask.

She sits up slightly and stares at me, her eyes darting between mine. I'm not sure what she's looking for, and I'm too emotionally drained to hide what I'm feeling, so I don't.

She brushes her thumb over my cheek like I've done so many times to her and then cups my jaw. "I'm in this, Trent. For the long haul. I'm going to tell Will. I know it's important to both of us that he knows. I just didn't want to add to his plate. I've really never seen him that bad before. His house was a disaster, and there were beer cans everywhere." She wrinkles her nose. "And he stunk like he hadn't showered in days. Will's not a vain guy, but he's always been clean. Who I saw tonight was not my brother." She stares intently in my eyes. "I promise I'll tell him once he's not such a mess."

"Okay."

There's nothing else to say. I have to trust her, and her eyes are shining with sincerity, not the insecurities I've seen in the past. I let it go, and we spend the rest of the night cuddled up on her couch until we both fall asleep. I'm so emotionally drained I expect to sleep deeply, but instead I wake up often throughout the night, pulling Becka a little tighter against me each time until she's practically draped on top of me. She hums softly and nuzzles her face against my chest, which eases some of the tightness in my body. By the time the sun starts to rise, my lids close heavily, and sleep consumes me, my last thought about Becka and how thankful I am that at least everything with us is fine.

29

Becka

The past month has gone by in a blur of prep for the release of the Rapturous Intent documentary, and I've felt like the worst sister because I've barely been able to check on Will. He started seeing his therapist again, which was a huge relief, but I still feel like I've failed him a little bit. Not to mention I still haven't told him about Trent, even though I'm feeling better than ever about our relationship. So when Will called me asking if I was free this afternoon, I made sure my schedule was cleared so I could get lunch with him.

I walk into my favorite restaurant in Santa Monica and immediately see my brother at a table near one of the front windows. I make my way through the nearly empty tables, grateful there aren't too many people here who might potentially recognize him. That's the downside of being related to someone mildly famous—we almost always get interrupted whenever we go out by someone asking for an autograph.

Although I suppose it's a blessing that I'm already used to that since it's a million times worse whenever Trent and I go out, even with his bodyguard running interference. Which is probably why he prefers to spend most of our time inside, which doesn't bother me in the slightest since that almost always leads to sexy times.

Shaking my head in an attempt to clear my suddenly dirty

thoughts, I get to the table at the same time that Will stands up to greet me with a hug. He looks so much better than the last time I saw him in person. His eyes are clear instead of vacant and haunted. His smile is present, albeit reserved, and he even looks healthier—his skin has a healthy glow about it instead of the sickly pallor he was sporting after he broke up with Gina.

"Thanks for coming," he says.

"Are you kidding? I feel terrible that it's taken us so long to get together. Work has been insane. We have that huge documentary releasing next week, and it's been nonstop PR." I don't mention that I've also spent every spare moment wrapped up in Trent. "So, how are you? You look a lot better than last time I saw you."

"I'm doing a lot better. Gina and I are back together, for good this time."

My lips quirk up in a soft smile, and I place my hand on his on top of the table. "I'm so happy to hear that, Will. So, I take it therapy helped."

"Yeah, and I won't be quitting this time. I'm still seeing my therapist, just not as frequently."

"Good, I'm glad."

He shifts in his seat, almost like he's uncomfortable. "I need to confess something to you, something I've never told you."

"Okay." I take a sip of my water, my throat suddenly dry and my palms damp from nerves.

He tells me about the guilt he carried over Candace's death, and the more he talks the more my gut clenches. How did I never realize he had all these demons tormenting him? How did I miss the signs that something more happened that night?

Tears fill my eyes as I realize how much my brother has suffered for years in silence. "Will...I can't believe you never told me."

"I know. I'm sorry, I just—"

"You have absolutely nothing to apologize for. I should've seen it. I know you. I should've realized there was more going on.

I'm so sorry I've been such a shitty sister." I hate all the pain my brother has gone through and that all this time I missed it.

"Becks. You are the opposite of a shitty sister. You've always been there for me when I needed you, without fail. I wasn't ready to share this. I never told anyone. My therapist was the first person I ever confessed it to, and it took weeks of intense therapy before I could finally say the words out loud."

"Does Gina know?"

"She does. She was the reason I finally dealt with all my ghosts. I knew if I wanted her to give me another shot, and for our relationship to work, I needed to deal with the one thing that was holding me back."

"I can't believe I never realized there was more to the story. I know you. I should've known something was up."

"This isn't on you at all. I wasn't ready to tell anyone, and I worked really hard to keep it hidden."

He says that, but I still feel like I should've known. And knowing I've kept something big from him only makes me feel a million times worse.

"I'm dating Trent." The words spew from my mouth like water out of a squirt gun, and his face is just as shocked and taken aback as if I'd actually sprayed water at his face.

He shakes his head, like he's not sure he heard me right. "Wait. Trent? As in our friend, Trent? Trent Bridger?"

I nod my head, my eyes wide and unblinking as I wait for him to yell at me. Instead he leans back in his chair and lets out a disbelieving laugh.

"Wow. I totally should've seen that coming."

Now it's my turn to be surprised. "What?"

He just looks at me like I should know what he's talking about. "Come on. There was always a weird vibe between you two. Even when we were all just friends, there was a chemistry there. I actually thought you two would start dating after he kissed you when you guys were fifteen, but then neither of you ever talked about it and then you ended up hanging with a different friend group more often than not, so I didn't bother bringing it up."

"Wait, hold up. You knew about that?"

"Of course I knew. Elise saw you two and blabbed to me and Lainey when you were at swim practice."

My jaw drops. "That little brat!"

Will just laughs. "How long have you two been dating?"

"Officially? Only a little over a month. I wanted to tell you when I last saw you, but you'd just broken up with Gina and you were…"

He waits for me to finish, but when I don't, he does it for me. "A complete mess."

"Something like that, yeah. I didn't want to add to your plate."

"And unofficially?"

"God, that's a long story."

"I have time."

So, I tell my brother all about how Trent and I first got together. Our rekindled friendship after years apart and then our night together, although I leave out the details because…yuck. I am not about to talk about my sex life with my brother.

When I finish, Will just smiles. "I'm happy for you two."

"You're not mad?"

He frowns. "Why would I be mad?"

I shrug. "Because Trent was more your friend than mine, at least after high school."

"Yeah, and he's a good guy. I know he'll be good to you. Hell, he gets my endorsement hands down over any of the other assholes you've dated in the past."

I roll my eyes, knowing he's not wrong, but not totally willing to admit it. Trent is definitely nothing like the guys I've dated before, which still scares me, especially the deeper we get.

Trent makes me feel things I thought were a myth, and a part of me is still wondering if the rug is going to get ripped out from under me.

"Do you think Gina's the one?" I ask.

Will's penetrating stare tells me he's not sure where I'm going with this subject change, but he answers nonetheless. "Yes."

"You can take a minute to think about it," I say, a little breathless that he was able to answer so quickly. Isn't he afraid she could leave him, or hurt him? What if he freaks out again? He didn't even take a second to think about that.

As if he can read my mind, he responds, "I've spent a lot of time thinking about it. All the time we were apart, in fact. Being without Gina was hell for me, a deeper hell than the one I'd been living in." He folds his hands and leans his elbows on the table. "I spent a lot of years letting my past dictate my future, and it didn't get me anywhere. Now that I'm working through all that, I finally feel like I can move forward with my life, and the only one I want to move forward with is Gina."

Picking at the cuticle on my thumb, I hesitate to ask him what I really want to know, but Will and I have kept enough from each other, and it's time we have an honest conversation. "Do you think Dad was part of the problem?"

He lets out a heavy sigh before answering. "A little, yeah. But it was mostly Candace. I got my closure with Dad after the draft." His gaze locks on mine. "But you've never gotten closure, have you?"

I shake my head, fighting against the pressure in my chest, and long-buried emotions battle inside me.

"Elise told me she was looking for him," I say and then nibble on my lip wondering if I should tell him that I want to find him too.

"She found him," he says.

My eyes widen in surprise, and my voice comes out hoarse. "What?"

"She called me last night because I asked her to tell me first if and where she found him. He's in Vegas. She wants to fly out and see him…well, more like confront him."

I should've known she'd find him. My little sister has always been tenacious, and now I know exactly who I'll be calling once I leave, since Elise hasn't called me yet. I know I need closure of some kind—if therapy has taught me anything so far, it's that. I'm just not sure what that'll look like.

I know that he's a big reason why I'm so afraid to trust my relationship with Trent. Which means if there's even a chance for Trent and me to have a real future together, then I need to face my past.

30

BECKA

Trent sits across from me at the conference table as we discuss our plans for the next week leading up to the release of the documentary. We've arranged several press events with the band, both private one-on-one meetings and two larger events that will be open to the public and everyone involved in the making of the documentary.

Normally, I'm the most focused person in the room, and given that I'm leading the charge on this one, I really should be. But Trent is sitting there looking fucking delicious in a tight-fitting black T-shirt that shows off the tattoos running up and down his arm and looking at me with heat in his eyes, like he's imagining me naked. Seeing as how he's seen me naked nearly every damn day, that's probably not hard for him.

What is hard is staying focused when he's so damn distracting. I'm struggling to remember that other people are in the room, and I can feel my cheeks heating in embarrassment when Megan, one of my team members, gently kicks me under the table. I break my gaze from Trent and realize it's my turn to speak.

Whoops.

"Okay," I say, clearing my throat and trying to dispel the lusty thoughts I was having about the sexy rock star whose grin tells me he knows exactly what I was thinking about. "So, we'll be doing a social media blitz."

"Will we get copies of that so I can get it on the band's social media pages?" Robbie asks.

"Yes. Megan will loop you in, so you'll get everything that'll be going out." Addressing the whole group, I continue, "You have an interview with *People Magazine* tomorrow morning. And another with *Entertainment Weekly* the following day. Those two are doing a lot of promotion with us, so make sure you shine in the interviews. We've also lined up several interviews with entertainment news stations at the red-carpet premiere that we're throwing. We'll need each of you at the designated spots for each interview. Penny," I say, gesturing to another member of my team, "will be on the red carpet directing you where to go, so just make sure you keep an eye out for her. Does anyone have any questions?"

Trent's eyes get dangerously seductive, and I'm pretty sure any questions he's thinking are sure to be dirty and not at all related to the premiere. I glance at Tristan, Kasen, Miles, and then Robbie, but they all shake their heads. I know their routine enough by now to know if they do have any questions, they'll pass them on to Robbie who will ask us. He's the unsung hero of the group, and it's almost a bummer he doesn't get more acclaim for how much the band relies on him.

"Great," Simone says. "Then you all are free to go, and we'll be in touch with you throughout the week leading up to the premiere. We're so excited about this, you guys. It's gonna be huge." Her smile is wide, but she looks at the guys with dollar signs in her eyes.

"We're excited too," Trent says, and then everyone gets up from the table and makes their way out. The buzz of several conversations fills the room as everyone leaves, but it's just background noise to my racing heart. I peek up at Trent and catch him already looking at me. When our gazes connect, his smile grows devious, and he arches a brow while sliding a finger across his lips like he's imagining all the different ways he can make me scream in pleasure.

Is it hot in here? Because suddenly I'm sweating, and there's a slickness between my thighs that was definitely not there twenty minutes ago.

"Becka, may I speak to you privately?" His voice is husky, and I'm relieved very few people that I work with are left in the room or they would for sure know that he's thinking dirty, dirty thoughts.

"Mmhmm." I can't say anything else, afraid my voice might crack. I stand up, grab my portfolio holding the agenda and all the other notes I needed for today's meeting, and make my way to my office. I don't look back to see if Trent is following me. I don't need to. He's so close I can feel the heat of his body at my back.

The door closes behind him, and the soft click of the lock is like a starter pistol starting a race. I spin around to find Trent already there, his hands in my hair and his lips slamming down on mine in an aggressive kiss that makes my toes curl in my shoes. Our hands are everywhere, quickly shedding our clothes while I try with every ounce of restraint I possess to remain quiet. His mouth drops small kisses along my jaw before he sucks on my neck, not enough to leave a mark, but enough to feel it between my legs. A groan escapes my throat.

"Shh," he whispers in my hair, his hot breath sending goosebumps across my skin. "If you're too loud, someone will come to check on you and then we'd have to stop. You don't want that, do you?"

"No," I say, my voice shaky and breathless.

"Good girl."

Oh God, why is that like striking a match to my libido? If I thought I hungered for him before, it's nothing compared to now. My fingers slide around his neck and bring his head down to mine so I can caress his lips with my own fierce and aggressive kiss. He makes a noise that's between a groan and a growl, and I smile to myself.

"Shh, you wouldn't want someone to hear, would you?" I say, throwing his words back to him. His eyes flash with heat and then he's stripping the last of my clothes off my body and hauling me up in his arms. He carries me over to my desk and places me on the edge, keeping his body wedged between my legs. He kisses me roughly again before grabbing a condom from his pants pocket, pushing his pants down, and sheathing his thick and hard cock faster than I can blink.

He slides inside me, and we both gasp and grip each other tight. Bliss rolls over my body in waves, already making my legs shake around him and my chest rise and fall in quick, shallow pants.

"Fuck, Becka," he whispers hoarsely along my neck, never once slowing down his thrusts.

I fight back the moan that is begging to be let out as he takes my body higher and higher until I'm sure if I don't come in the next thirty seconds, I'll die.

"Come for me," he says at the same time he slides his hand between us and rubs his thumb over my clit.

His steady, rough thrusts and the quick frantic motion of his thumb against my clit trigger my climax. I detonate around him on a gasp that's aching to be a scream, and my thighs clench against his hips, shaking from the intensity of my release. With one more thrust, he comes with me, his body shaking as he tries to hold his lower half still against me. A shiver rolls down his spine and then his gaze is locked on mine, and there's so much in his eyes that matches how I'm feeling that it leaves me breathless.

He brushes a lock of hair behind my ear, and then holds my cheek. "I love you, Becka."

Now I'm breathless for a completely different reason. "What?"

He smiles—my smile, not his rock star one—and says, "You heard me, but I'm happy to repeat myself." He drops his forehead to mine and breathes me in. "I love you. You own me, heart, body, and soul. I'm yours."

I swear my heart is going to beat out of my chest, and tears threaten the backs of my eyes. "I love you too."

"I know."

I slap his arm, and he lets out a laugh that causes my own face to break out into an exuberant grin. "You're such a smart-ass."

"Only with you," he says, dropping a kiss to my lips that I take all too willingly.

We pull apart and get dressed, knowing that we're pushing the boundaries before someone comes looking for me for a work-related issue.

When we're both dressed, Trent surprises me. "So, you gonna tell me what happened yesterday?"

"What do you mean?"

"I mean, you didn't want me to come over last night after you saw Will. Did he take it badly? Is that why?"

"No," I say, straightening out my desk and wishing I could just as easily straighten out the thoughts in my head. I was in a weird headspace after seeing Will and just needed a night alone to process it all. "Will's actually really happy for us."

Trent places his hands on his hips and watches me carefully. "Okay, then what's the problem?"

I inhale deeply and then blow out a heavy breath, wanting to tell him everything but also afraid to be vulnerable. I shouldn't still be afraid after we just said "I love you" for the first time, but I've also never been as open with a boyfriend as I am with Trent.

Everything's different with Trent.

"Elise found our dad, and I think maybe I need some closure with him so I don't end up ruining this," I say, gesturing between us.

His gaze softens, and he walks toward me until I'm wrapped in his arms, my head resting on his chest where I can hear the steady thrum of his heartbeat beneath his clothes. "You aren't going to ruin this or run me off. Trust me, I'm not going anywhere, except on tour in the future, but I'm not letting you go again, got it?"

I nod and wrap my arms around his hips, not ready for him to pull away, wishing I was as confident in myself as he is.

With one more tender kiss, I let him go and walk with him to my door. He gives my hand a squeeze before he opens the door, and I lean against the doorjamb watching his sexy ass strut down the hall, my heart fluttering with the knowledge that he is all mine. It's when I turn to go back to my office that familiar brown eyes meet mine before glancing behind me where I know Trent is still likely visible. Brad's coffee-colored gaze shoots back to mine, a question in his eyes that I refuse to acknowledge, instead going into my office and closing the door.

My hope that he'll ignore what he thinks he saw quickly evaporates when he knocks once on my door and then opens it before I've even told him he can come in.

I turn on my heels and cross my arms, glaring at him for his arrogance of storming into my office without an invitation.

"I have work to do. What do you want?" My voice could freeze the Pacific Ocean with the arctic chill it's giving off.

Clearly unfazed, he puts on a small smile, the same one that used to endear him to me. "We haven't talked in a while. How are you?"

My glare sharpens. We both know what he saw—Trent coming out of my office looking not quite as put-together as he was when he walked in—so I'm not sure what game he's playing at here.

Instead of taking my silence as a sign he should get out, he takes a step closer, his expression turning serious. "Becka, I know I messed things up with how I handled our breakup and not warning you about my engagement to Shelly. It was unexpected, to me more than anyone. But I still care about you."

I fight back the eye roll that I want to let loose.

Undeterred, he continues. "You should be careful with him."

My blood boils. How fucking dare he! "Excuse me," I say, my voice ice while my skin feels like it's on fire. Who the hell does he think he is?

"Have you watched the cut footage of the RI documentary?"

"Why would I? I only watch what goes out for publicity purposes."

He nods like that's what he suspected. "I think you need to see something." He turns and heads to my door, halfway out before he realizes I'm not following him.

"Becka?"

"I have no desire to see anything you have to show me. You can close the door."

His eyebrows furrow in confusion and then consternation. "Now you're just being stubborn. I'm telling you that guy can't be trusted. I saw the footage from the tour. *All* the footage. Trust me, there's definitely something you're going to want to see."

Walking to my door, I grab the handle. "I don't trust you and haven't for a long time. Don't bother coming back to my office. You have nothing I want." Then, I slam the door in his shocked face, vindication thrumming through my veins.

But an hour later, that vindication evaporates when Brad sends me an email with footage attached and one sentence. *Trust me or don't, but you deserve to know.*

Doubt niggles the back of my mind, and before I can talk myself out of it, I press play and feel the metaphorical rug get ripped out from under me.

31

Becka

I've spent the last several days in a daze, throwing myself into work until my eyes felt like sand and my eyelids were so heavy that I had no other choice but to fall asleep the second my head hit the pillow.

But tonight's the documentary premiere, and I won't be able to avoid him for much longer.

I've had that damn video burned into my brain since I watched it. Women throwing their panties at the band, then draping themselves all over the guys backstage. While Trent wasn't in too much of that specific footage, there was plenty of footage of gorgeous woman after gorgeous woman flirting with him backstage and asking him to sign their cleavage during VIP meet and greets.

It's one thing to think you know what goes on during tour—it's a whole other story actually seeing it.

There's a part of my brain that understands I'm pulling away again, but Brad hit on the nerve of all my insecurities.

Can I really be enough for a guy like Trent?

He could have any woman he wants. Why would he want someone as broken and messed up as me? All the months of therapy feel like a waste as I slip back into old habits—ignoring the part of my brain that's trying to be rational and forcing me to really think this through.

I just need to get through this premiere and then I can sit down with my therapist and have her talk me off this ledge that I'm standing on.

Fans are already lining the red carpet, eagerly awaiting the arrival of the band, when I get there and finalize the interview details with Penny before sending her off to meet with the entertainment reporters. Deafening screams break out, and my skin prickles with awareness.

He's here.

I turn around just in time to catch a glimpse of him from my spot tucked back behind all the craziness. My heart clenches, and doubt creeps in that I've messed this up. What am I thinking? That gorgeous man just confessed that he loves me. I'm being crazy.

I'm about to walk over to him when someone grabs my elbow, and I turn to see Simone standing there staring at me with surprise.

"What are you doing here? I thought you would've been out celebrating by now?"

"What are you talking about?"

"Your promotion! Why are you still working? Marshall said you could take the night off. Hell, you've earned it."

Oh yes, the promotion I worked so hard for that felt bittersweet when I actually got it this morning because the first person I wanted to tell was the same person I was avoiding.

"What can I say? I'm a workaholic."

"Clearly," she says, shaking her head at me like she thinks I'm crazy.

Get in line, sister.

Gesturing behind me I say, "I'm going to go check on the band. Make sure everything's running smoothly."

She smiles knowingly at me and then I turn to make my escape, only to see Trent smiling down at a fan with a softness in his gaze that causes me to suck in a breath. Instead of continuing forward, I stop and watch him interacting with the beautiful bevy of women standing in front of him.

My doubts creep back in, and without thinking it through too much I turn back to Simone. "Actually, I think I will take the night off. I'm also going to need the next few days. There's something I need to do that requires me to leave town," I tell her, an idea already forming in my head.

"Everything okay?"

"Yeah, just family stuff."

"Okay, not a problem. Things should be pretty quiet. All the feedback has been positive so far, so even if we get any bad reviews, I'm sure we can handle it."

"Great," I say and then hustle out of there, my heels clacking loudly against the cement of the sidewalk in my haste to get to my car.

On my drive home, I call Elise.

"Hey, Becks, what's up?"

"Let's go see Dad."

"That's what we've already planned."

I shake my head even though she can't see me. "No, I mean, let's go tomorrow."

She hesitates before responding. "Tomorrow? Why the sudden urgency?"

Because I need answers. I need to know why I wasn't enough for him to stick around. I need to know if I'll always be broken. "Because I have a few days off."

She's silent so long, I worry she's going to tell me no, when she finally says, "Okay. I just found a flight from Austin to Vegas that arrives tomorrow morning at nine a.m. Can you meet me there?"

A huge sigh of relief escapes me. "Done. I'll text you my flight info once I get it booked."

"See you tomorrow."

We hang up, and I feel like at least I have something under control. That is, until I'm home packing and get a text from Trent.

TRENT

> Hey gorgeous, where are you?

My gut clenches with a mix of guilt, longing, and regret.

ME

> I'm at home. Something came up with Elise and I've got to go out of town for a few days.

I nibble my lip, waiting for his response.

TRENT

> What's going on?

ME

> Just family stuff.

He responds almost instantly.

TRENT

> Why are you being vague? What's wrong?

I should've known that wouldn't be enough for him. I've been making excuses for days, blaming work on why we couldn't see each other. Of course he's not going to be satisfied with my weak answers.

ME

> Nothing.

TRENT

> Bullshit.

I start to text him another excuse when I pause, my heart aching with the realization of what I really need to do. I start and delete multiple drafts before I finally compose something that I can send to him. That rational part of my brain screams at me again, but the little girl that lives inside me, heartbroken and lost, wins out like she always does.

ME

> I can't do this anymore. I'm sorry. I thought I could, but I think it's too much for me.

I wait for a response. For him to fight me on it. But the text never comes, and by the time I realize I've made a mistake, I know it's too late. I've pushed him too far.

32

TRENT

The cushion of the chair gives under the weight of my body as I finally take a seat in the auditorium that is quickly filling up with patrons all here to see the premiere of our documentary. I heave a sigh of relief that we've made it this far.

This night has been exhausting—from the hours it took to get ready, interview after interview on the red carpet, and the constant barrage of fans and flashing lights from paparazzi. I've spent most of the day torn between worrying about Kasen and dying to see Becka.

We've been going nonstop for days, meeting with every press person in the state of California—or at least that's what it feels like. But the endless hours of torture answering the same questions over and over again are nothing compared to the nights without Becka in my arms.

She's been slammed with work getting everything done for the documentary premiere, and despite my constant efforts, our schedules never seem to match up. I'm trying not to be that clingy guy, but I miss my girl.

I'm so glad it's opening night, and I'll finally get to sleep with her tucked in my arms again where she belongs.

Kasen is another story altogether. Miles, Tristan, Robbie, and I have rotated who's on duty watching him. Robbie took over for the premiere, but it didn't escape my notice how antsy Kasen was during the red-carpet interviews. He was glued to his phone the whole drive over here, and all I kept wondering was if he was texting Charli. Based on the worried glances I caught Miles and Tristan shooting his way, I wasn't the only one with that concern.

I wasn't sure how he'd do during the interviews, but it seems like he pulled it together enough to get through them. He's a lot calmer now, and it kills me that my first thought is that somehow he was able to sneak a hit of something without us noticing.

We need to have another conversation about what the long-term plan will be to support him because what we're doing now isn't sustainable. But that's a worry for another day.

Right now, all I want is to see Becka and finally feel the serenity that only she can give me. I glance around the room, recognizing some of the faces of those here to see the premiere—other celebrities as well as execs from VibeTV and the PR team we've been working with. But there's no sign of Becka anywhere.

I'm not ashamed to say I'm getting desperate to see her. This is the longest we've been apart since we got together after my tour, and I don't like it.

Right before the documentary is supposed to start, I cave and ask Penny when she walks past where I'm sitting.

"Hey, Penny, where's Becka? She's here tonight, right?"

Penny's sharp gaze scans the audience, a furrow in her brow. "Yeah, she should be. I thought I saw her earlier talking to Simone, but now that you mention it, I haven't seen her since."

I glance around the room, my gut starting to feel unsettled. I think back to the last time I saw Becka—when we had a quickie in her office a few days ago. Nothing was amiss when I left. She had a smile on her face and that just-fucked look in her eyes that I've become addicted to.

No signs of anything brewing in that beautiful, wonderful, overthinking brain of hers. I thank Penny, and when she walks away, I pull out my phone and send Becka a text. I'm not going to play games with her.

My knee bounces restlessly as I wait for her to respond. When my phone buzzes in my hand, I react like an addict eager for my next hit, quickly clicking on her message and reading it, searching for answers that it doesn't reveal.

I text her again and my brow instantly furrows in concern when she responds with another similarly vague answer. Frustration joins the concern brewing in my gut as she dodges my questions with mostly one-word answers. Until finally she sends a blow that I should've seen coming.

> **BECKA**
>
> I can't do this anymore. I'm sorry. I thought I could, but I think it's too much for me.

I don't respond. I know better. Something happened, and I'll figure out what the hell it was because no way in hell am I losing this woman. I love her enough to love her through her crazy irrational freak-outs. She's going to have to do a whole hell of a lot more than that if she thinks she can drive me away.

Just as the lights dim around the room signaling the start of the documentary, I shoot off one more text, to Will this time.

If Becka won't tell me what's going on, then I'll find out another way.

33

Becka

The plane lands and my heart drops with it. I'm way more nervous than I thought I was going to be, and I'm having a hard time getting out of my head. I also can't help but feel like I left my world in shambles back in LA.

But there's no point thinking about that when I can only focus on one problem at a time right now.

I find Elise at baggage claim, texting on her phone.

"Hey, stranger," I say, my voice clogging with emotion because I haven't seen her in almost a year, and I've missed her like crazy.

Her wavy brown hair is shorter than when I saw her last, now cut so it rests at the top of her shoulders. Her green eyes—an Edmonson trait we all inherited—sparkle when she sees me, and she jumps up from her chair and rushes over to me. We embrace in a tight hug, and when we part there are a few stray tears in both our eyes.

"I've missed you, Becks."

"I've missed you too," I say, pulling her in for another tight hug. Sometimes it's hard not to still see the little girl in pigtails who cut my favorite Barbie's hair because she wanted to be a hair stylist and thought it would grow back. But I can't deny that the poised young woman in front of me is no longer that little girl.

She's all grown up now, and I couldn't be prouder of the woman she's become.

She pulls back, and her warm expression turns cautious and serious. "You ready for this?"

Isn't that the million-dollar question?

"As ready as I'll ever be, I guess."

"Me too."

"Then what are we waiting for? Let's get this over with."

The ride to the hotel is a blur, my head torn between two unknowns, one awaiting us here in Vegas and the one I left behind. We get checked in, drop off our luggage, and then head back down to the lobby, never really taking a moment to rest. I don't know Elise's reasons, but I imagine they're similar to mine. I have to keep moving, or I'm afraid I'll chicken out.

We make our way out of the hotel, and after glancing down at her phone, Elise looks around.

"There are some cabs over there," I say, pointing to a line of yellow taxi cabs.

Elise ignores me, and then her gaze settles on a black town car and she smiles wide. "No need for a cab. That's our ride," she says, pointing to the town car, which has to cost way more than a cab.

"Uh, are you sure? Let's just take a cab. It's cheaper."

Once again, she ignores me, making her way to the car, and like the loyal sister I am, I follow her. If that's how she wants to waste her money, then who am I to stop her?

When we get inside the air-conditioned car, I take a sigh of relief to be out of the oppressive Vegas heat.

"What made you want to rent a town car?"

She doesn't look at me, her gaze taking in the scenery outside the window as she responds. "It just seemed like a good idea."

I stare at the side of her head until she closes her eyes and lets out a heavy breath in exasperation. She turns her green gaze toward me and takes in my disbelieving expression.

"Fine. I didn't want us to have to deal with following directions in an unfamiliar place or stressing out about getting lost, or worse being too emotional to drive, depending on how things turn out. So that meant renting a car was out, and cabs aren't always reliable, so this just seemed like the best solution." She pauses, and a coy smile lifts her lips. "Besides, I got a hell of a deal, and it's hardly costing me a thing."

"If you insist."

"I do," she says and then leans forward to give the driver the address to our dad's house.

The wheels roll underneath us as we pass the sights of the strip where we're staying and head toward Henderson where my dad lives. The air conditioning blows through the car, sending goosebumps across my arm and juxtaposing the suffocating heat I know waits outside the comfort of our vehicle. The tan terrain passes us by, and if I loved brown, I could find it beautiful. But there's something so desolate about it that I find myself missing the blue of the ocean I can see from my condo.

"Are you nervous?" Elise whispers next to me.

Turning to her, I see her looking out at the landscape just like I was. "I think we'd be crazy not to be. It's been a long time since we've seen him."

"Do you think he ever thinks of us?" she asks, turning her gaze from the view outside to meet mine. There's a tension around her eyes that I'm sure matches my own.

"I don't know, but we're about to find out."

Before I'm ready, the driver turns into a residential neighborhood. My body tenses, and my blood heats as I watch house after house become bigger and more gorgeous the farther into the neighborhood we go. With two more turns, the driver slows in front of a stucco house with a rounded clay tile roof. There's a beautifully landscaped lawn, palm trees, and a three-car garage. Elise and I both stare out at the house that's probably more than three times the size of the small house we lived in after our dad left us.

I fight back the rage that's threatening to curdle my blood. He left us in poverty and has been living a life of luxury this whole time?

What the actual fuck?

Elise turns to me, her expression unsure but fortitude in her gaze. She looks back out the window, takes a deep breath, and then opens the door and steps out.

"I can do this," I whisper to myself, while also wishing I had asked Trent to come with me. That I hadn't been so scared that I let my crazy get the better of me. The resolve to fix things with him moves swiftly through me, and I'm more determined than ever to make things right for good with him.

No matter what happens with my dad today, I'm done running away from my fears and letting my insecurities rule my life.

I open my own door, slide out, and then walk around the car until I'm standing next to Elise, both of us staring at this house with dismay, and a slew of other emotions far too complicated and long-buried to name in this moment.

With a deep breath, I walk toward the door, carefully placing one foot in front of the other and fighting every instinct in my body telling me this is a bad idea. It's time to face my dad.

I stop at the front door and feel more than see Elise stop next to me. My gaze is locked on the door, my vision so focused on what could be on the other side that I can't even turn to look at my sister to see how she's feeling.

"This feels like a slap in the face," she says, her voice scratchier than it was in the car, and I know she's fighting back angry tears. "Mom deserves a house like this, not Dad."

"She has a house like this, thanks to Will." My brother bought our mom a nice house in Austin when he got his first big signing bonus.

"Maybe this was a mistake."

I break from my stare off with the front door and turn a sharp eye to my sister. "You're having second thoughts."

It's not a question.

"Aren't you? I mean, look at this? He's clearly not lacking for anything and yet he's never reached out to either of us."

I reach out and grab her hand, squeezing it gently. "We've come too far to turn back now. We need to see this through and then be done with him for good. We're strong, and we deserve to have this conversation with him. Even if it's just seeing him face-to-face and getting the closure we deserve."

She stares at me for a few blinks before nodding her head swiftly, turning toward the front door and ringing the doorbell. We can hear the loud chime from out here as well as a dog barking somewhere inside the house. A man shouts at the dog to be quiet; my heart speeds up, and my stomach tightens painfully. Nerves make my hands clammy, but I don't even have time to wipe them on my shorts before the door opens, and he's standing there in front of us.

I've seen his picture enough times to recognize him, although he's grayed to the point of salt and pepper now. He's still in decent shape for his age and wears a pair of khaki shorts and a light blue golf polo.

He smiles at us both, his eyes lighting up, but not in recognition. "Can I help you lovely ladies?"

Elise opens her mouth to speak, but her eyes are wide, and I think she might be slightly in shock because she doesn't get any words out. I step forward and stick my hand out. "I'm Becka and this is Elise. We're your daughters."

His smile vanishes instantly, and his gaze turns questioning as he now appraises us like he's trying to figure out why we're standing at his front door.

Frankly, I'm starting to wonder the same thing.

He crosses his arms over his chest and stares at us. "What are you girls doing here?"

"We were hoping we could talk to you," Elise says, finally finding her voice.

"About what?"

She swallows and glances at me, unsure, before facing our dad again. "We have some questions. Do you have a minute?"

"Now's not a good time."

"It won't take long," I say. "We don't have any intention of sticking around, but I think after over twenty years of being a deadbeat dad, we deserve a few minutes of your time."

He glares at me but doesn't say anything, and after what feels like an eternity, he takes a step back and gestures inside. I walk in, my head held high and my shoulders back like my hands aren't shaking with nerves. Elise follows me, and we head into his living room. My jaw drops when I see how nice the inside of his house is.

From the foyer, we can see what looks like a formal living room with a beautiful chandelier. Down the hall, I can see part of the kitchen and what looks like high-end stainless steel appliances and white-and-gray marble countertops. Everything is spotless, and while I've seen fancier houses in California, this is still so much more than I had growing up. I'm having a hard time reconciling the fact that my dad left us in poverty and has essentially been living a life of luxury, even if he's probably only solid upper-middle class. I'm having trouble catching my breath, but like hell I'm going to let him see me as weak.

"So what's this about?" he asks, joining us in the living room and gesturing for us to take a seat.

Elise and I look to each other as we sit down, and it's clear from the shocked and saddened look in her eyes that she still held out hope that this would be a happy reunion.

I held no such expectations.

"We have some questions for you," I say, ready to move things along.

His eyes turn to slits as he watches us carefully. "What kinds of questions?"

"Why did you leave?" Elise spits out in one quick breath that I'm pretty sure she holds waiting for his answer.

He sits back in his chair and crosses his arms, his stare still calculating. "Because I wanted to."

That...was not the answer I was expecting.

I was expecting him to say some bullshit like he wasn't cut out for fatherhood, or he needed a change, or he freaked out, but to hear that he left simply because he *wanted* to feels like the biggest slap in the face yet. A glance to Elise and her parted mouth, wide eyes brimming with tears and heartbreak written all over her face, tells me that wasn't the answer she was expecting either.

"Did you ever think about what we—your kids—might want? That we might want our dad around?" I ask.

He rolls his eyes. "Your mom could handle you. She's the one who wanted kids anyway."

"You didn't want kids?" Elise's voice cracks, and I wish I could shield her from his venom.

"Of course not. Kids were never in the cards for me. I tried it because I loved your mom, but after we had the last one, I knew that wasn't the life I wanted."

The last one, like he doesn't know that Elise is his youngest child—or I hope she is his last child. God knows what he's gotten up to in the last twenty-two years.

Elise stands up abruptly, a torrent of tears cascading down her face. "I've heard enough," she says, her voice hollow, and then storms out of the house. I watch her go, knowing I'll follow shortly, but I have a few more questions and I never want to see this man again, so I need to make this visit count.

"You said you loved my mom, but you still left."

"I did."

"Why did you leave her if you loved her?"

I hold my breath waiting for his response. Somehow it feels like his answer will unlock the truth about why men have always found it so easy to leave me. Or it might explain my need to leave them as soon as my insecurities get the better of me, something I wasn't even fully aware of until I started therapy—although it didn't stop me from having that knee-jerk reaction with Trent yesterday. Once again, the need to fix things with him surfaces as I face the man who made me this way.

"Because, as it turns out, I didn't love her. I wasn't willing to give up the life I really wanted for the one she wanted, so I left. She wanted you kids. I didn't."

"You only ever loved yourself," I say, my own voice coming out soft while my brain wraps around his response.

He shrugs. "If you want to look at it that way, sure. But I have no regrets. I'm sure that's not what you want to hear, but I'm living the life I want."

"I just wanted the truth. Thank you for your time." I don't bother with other pleasantries because there's no point. He has no regrets, so neither will I. I stand up and walk out of his house, closing the door tightly behind me.

I lean against the wall beside the door for just a minute, closing my eyes and attempting to catch my breath and control the barrage of emotions. Despite how little time we spent with him, I think I got exactly what I needed from him.

It was never about me not being enough.

He simply wasn't enough.

He wasn't man enough to be there for his wife and kids.

He wasn't man enough to own his responsibilities.

He wasn't man enough to be a dad instead of simply a sperm donor.

But none of that was my fault.

Feeling my heart steady as I get the closure I was so desperate for, I open my eyes, and my breath immediately catches in my throat when I see the most beautiful pair of blue eyes staring back at me in concern.

"Are you okay? I was two seconds away from storming the house after the way Elise flew out of there crying." His arms wrap around me, and he pulls me against his chest, and I'm convinced I have to be dreaming. Trent can't actually be here right now, can he? The steady thrum of his heart lulls me into the safety of his embrace, and tears of relief prick my eyes. I didn't mess it up.

He's here for me, even after I tried to break up with him in a fit of crazy insecurity. I wrap my arms around his waist and hold him as close as I can. I love this man so much. I can't believe I almost lost this.

For the first time since our relationship started, a true sense of peace washes over me. This is real. This is love. Trent wants me—he's made that abundantly clear. And I want him. More than I've ever wanted anyone in my entire life.

"You won't leave me," I whisper on a soft sigh, my body suddenly feeling light and free.

Trent pulls back, frustration clear in the furrow of his brow. "I've told you I'm not going anywhere. You can push me away all you want, but I know you don't mean it. I love you, Becka. You're it for me."

34

TRENT

I don't know how many times I have to tell this woman I won't leave her before she finally believes me.

Relief shines in her eyes. "I love you too. I'm so sorry about everything that happened in LA. I just...Brad showed me some footage of the tour and girls all over you, and I just lost it."

I pull back more to stare in her eyes so I can better understand. "Brad? The douchebag you were crying over when we first bumped into each other?"

She nibbles her lip and nods her head.

"I don't know what footage he showed you, but I can assure you there was no one else on that tour. Besides hanging with the guys, I was by myself." I press my forehead to hers, trying to figure out how to prove to her that she's the only woman I want—the only one I will *ever* want. "Why didn't you talk to me about it?"

Her watery gaze meets with mine, and there's so much vulnerability there. "Honestly?"

"That'd be nice."

She lets out a shaky breath. "Because I didn't think I could be enough for you." She shakes her head like she thinks the thought is crazy—because it is. "I know that's not true now, but at the time, it just hit a nerve. I think maybe I was also feeling extra insecure because I knew Elise had found our dad, and I got lost in my own head about how if I wasn't good enough for him then how could I ever be good enough for you?"

"Becka, you are more than enough. You're enough when you're carefree and happy. You're enough when you're emotional and moody. You're enough when you're crazy and irrational. You are enough, always."

Tears slip down her cheeks as she chokes out, "I'm so sorry, Trent. I want to fix things with us. I don't want to lose you. I'm done letting my fears and insecurities get in the way."

Wiping the tears with my thumbs, I brush her lips with mine. "Good, because you're the love of my life, Becka. I can't live without you, nor do I want to."

She wraps her arms tighter around me, and we stand there holding each other for several minutes before I feel her body truly relax against me.

Brushing her hair, I ask, "Did you get what you needed from him?"

She looks up at me, her green eyes causing my heart rate to spike like it always does whenever she's near. "You know what? I did. I mean, he didn't really say much, but what he did say filled in some of the blanks that I've been living with my whole life."

I brush a lock of hair from her face and lean down to kiss her forehead, wanting any excuse to touch her. "Good. Then I'm glad you came."

"How did you know where I was?"

"Elise. I've been texting her since you tried to break up with me. Will gave me her number, and I reached out to her asking what was going on. She filled me in on all the details, and I organized the town car for you guys."

She pulls back. "Wait, you got us the town car?"

"Yeah. I didn't want you to have to worry about anything while you were dealing with your dad."

"And then you followed me here," she says, her contemplative gaze putting all the pieces together.

I nod, unashamed. I would do it again in a heartbeat. I'd do anything for her.

"Thank you," she says before leaning up to kiss me.

None of the Edmonson kids ever talked about their dad growing up. I asked Will about him once, and he said he wasn't worth the breath it would take to talk about him. So I never broached the subject again.

But things are different now. I have a lot of questions about him, and I want to be sure she's gotten all the closure she needs so she never has to deal with him again.

"Can you tell me a little about him?"

She glances back at the door she walked out of. "I honestly don't remember him. I only vaguely remembered what he looked like from pictures I'd seen, but I was four when he left and sometimes I think I remember things, but they're so indistinct I can't be sure. But I remember after. I remember all the nights my mom cried in her room or the bathroom thinking we didn't know. I remember her working herself to the bone so she could provide for us and still somehow finding ways to support us and read us bedtime stories and be there for us. I remember the first time someone asked me when I was in kindergarten why my dad didn't live with us. I didn't know. I didn't know why he'd left, but I kept thinking maybe it was my fault. Was I not good enough for him to stay? Was I not good enough for him to be my dad? He never sent birthday cards, or Christmas cards, or anything to let us know he even thought about us. It was like he just walked out the door and no longer existed. But we knew he was out there. I remember trying to be the best at whatever I tried because I thought maybe then he'd come around, he'd come watch me compete or something."

She competed in swim team until junior year. Will never told me why she quit, but now I wonder how much of why she even started was attributed to her dad.

"I remember the first father-daughter dance. Our grandparents had already passed, and my mom hadn't started dating Doug yet. I wanted to go so desperately, but I was the girl without a dad. Will offered to take me, but I couldn't bear the thought of being different from everyone else. I just wanted my dad. I wanted some sign he cared. I wanted him to want me."

Her voice doesn't crack like I expect it to. Instead, she holds her head up tall, her shoulders back and her body carrying a strength I don't know that I've ever seen in her before. She has to be the most beautiful woman in the world in this moment—hell, in every moment—but I'm admittedly biased.

"I don't need him to want me anymore in order to feel like I'm worthy. It was never about me to begin with. All his choices are on him." Her gaze drops to the ground briefly before looking up at me. "Just like my choices are mine." She brushes her hand against my jaw, and I fight the urge to close my eyes because it feels so good to have her touching me. "I made the wrong choice yesterday in LA, but I promise you I won't make that choice again. I choose you, Trent. From today on, I'll always choose you."

Pulling her close to me again because I simply can't stop touching her, I whisper against her hair. "I love you, Becka Edmonson, and I promise to choose you too. Always."

She stares at me in wonder. "Where did you come from?"

I can't help smirking, but I don't say anything snarky or cute like I usually would, because I know there's more she needs to let out. Hell, a lot of what she's said has stirred up memories of my own childhood and the feelings of abandonment and neglect I felt from my mom.

Quietly, she confesses, "I think I've spent most of my life expecting men to leave me because if the one man who's supposed to love me unconditionally didn't stay, why would anyone else?"

I can't take it anymore. Cupping her face, I bring her lips to mine and kiss her fiercely, needing to connect with her this way, to make sure she knows she's not alone. But the act itself isn't enough. "I'm not leaving you."

She looks at me, her green eyes still a little watery and her voice hoarse. "I want to believe you."

"I'll find a way to prove it, because I swear to you, Becka, you're it for me. I'm never letting you go. I don't want you to be waiting for the other shoe to drop. There's no other shoe. I'll have to literally leave for tours and stuff, but I'll always belong to you. There won't be any other women but you. For as long as I live, I'm yours."

Something shifts in her gaze and then her mouth is on mine, kissing me with a hunger that leaves me wanting more than just her lips. But now's not the time. Reluctantly, I break the kiss, leaning my forehead on hers as we both take deep breaths.

"I don't want to mess this up again, Trent."

"You won't. Because no matter what, I'll always be here waiting for you."

God, this woman. She has no idea what she means to me, even after all this time. Somehow all that I've said and done hasn't gotten through to her, and I'm not sure what it'll take, but I'll do anything to make sure she understands that there's nothing in this world she could ever do to drive me away.

Pulling away, she says, "Let's go to the car. I need to check on Elise."

We walk back to the car hand in hand, and when we get to the back doors, I release her, but not before dropping a too-brief kiss on her lips. She smiles softly, her eyes crinkling at the corners, and then slides in next to her sister. They immediately start murmuring to each other, and I know she'll spend the whole ride back to the hotel comforting Elise. I slide into the front passenger seat and let the driver know we're good to go.

It's still bothering me that somewhere in her head she thinks I might leave her, and the drive back gives me time to figure out how I'm going to convince Becka that I'm fully committed to her.

As we pass business after business and head closer to the strip,

I see something that immediately catches my eye, and instantly I know what I need to do. The idea should terrify me. I'm sure my brother would think I'm being reckless and insane, but it feels right. It feels so right that I'm antsy to get back to the hotel and put my plan in motion.

When the driver pulls up to the hotel, I tell him to wait because I have one more stop to make. I help Becka out of the car, while she holds hands with a more composed Elise, although her eyes are still red-rimmed from crying.

"I gotta run a quick errand. Why don't you spend some more time with Elise until I get back?"

"That would be great actually. I know she's going to want some alone time eventually to fully decompress, but the big sister in me isn't quite ready to leave her alone."

I give her another kiss—fighting against every urge in my body to make it more—and the spare key to my suite, so we can meet there later, and then get back in the car. Once the girls walk through the sliding double doors of the hotel, I turn to my driver.

"Take me to the best jeweler in Vegas."

I pace the floor of my suite waiting for Becka to return from Elise's room, the ring I just dropped an insane amount of money on burning a hole in my pocket. I called her as soon as I got back, and she said she'd be right up, but that was ten minutes ago.

What's taking her so long?

I'm antsy and dying to pour my heart out to her. I even wrote her a song in the car—the words coming to me swiftly and more clearly than any song I've ever written—but I thought that might be cheesy, so instead the lyrics are tucked in my pocket, and I'll save it as a surprise for later. I hear the buzz of the lock before the door swings open and in walks the absolute love of my life.

Fuck, she's gorgeous.

How the hell did I get so lucky?

Unable to stop myself, I move toward her and pull her into my arms, my lips finding hers in a salacious kiss. She moans softly and then wraps her arms tighter around me. Our tongues duel for dominance, and I know if I let this kiss continue, we'll be naked in no time and there's something much more important I want to do first.

Breaking the kiss, I step back slightly but still keep Becka in my arms. Her green eyes are slightly dazed and unfocused, and I love that I do that to her.

"I love you, Becka."

Her lips tilt up at the corners, and her eyes go soft. "I love you too, Trent. I know I've already said it once today, but thank you for following me here, for knowing what I needed even when I didn't."

"I'll follow you anywhere. Always." I place my hands on the side of her neck and tilt her head up so she's looking at me. "I'm not going anywhere. I'll prove it to you."

My heart speeds up until it's a stampede of rhinos in my chest, but I feel more excitement than nerves. She might think I'm completely crazy, but I've never been surer of anything in my life. I pull the ring box out of my pocket and get down on one knee. Her hands immediately cover her mouth, and her eyes go wide.

"Oh my God, Trent, what are you doing?"

I take her left hand and hold it tight. "I'm in this, Becka. I want to do life with you. The good and bad, the highs and lows. I want it all, but only with you. Only ever with you. I belong to you, Becka. I'm yours. You own me heart, body, and soul, and I want to spend the rest of my life by your side. Will you marry me?"

Her eyes fill with tears as she stares at me in shock, but then her lips tilt up slightly and she whispers, "Oh my God, I must be crazy." And I know what her answer will be.

She nods her head once and then lets out a laugh and wraps

her arms around my neck. "Yes," she whispers in my ear. "We're probably certifiably insane, but my answer is yes."

"There's no one else I'd rather be insane with."

She laughs again and then I slide the ring on her finger, and it feels real. She's going to be my wife. This isn't just a dream.

"Let's get married now."

"What?" she asks breathlessly.

"Let's do it here, in Vegas. There are a ton of places on the strip, and I don't want to wait. I mean, if you want a big fancy wedding then we can of course wait, but I want to be married to you. I want the whole world to see your ring on my finger and know I'm taken."

"I thought you weren't that reckless rock star anymore."

"This isn't being reckless. I love you, Becka. I spent eight months without talking to you, seeing you, touching you, and they were the worst eight months of my life. I've known since the moment I held you in my arms again that you were it for me. So why wait? Why wait to start my life with the woman of my dreams when I could start it right now? Jump with me, Becka. Take a risk. I won't let you fall. I'll spend every day of my life proving my vows to you. Say yes. Say you'll marry me, here, today, and we can start our lives together knowing we're in this together. Partners for life."

"But what about your brother? Won't he want to be here? And my family will be so mad at me if I get married without them."

"Forget about everyone else for a second. Do you want to get married today?"

She watches me, her eyes not giving away how she's feeling. I'll be okay with whatever she decides because she's already agreed to marry me, but I'm ready now. I'd marry her in the next ten minutes if she gave me the go-ahead. And not just to prove to her that I'm sticking around, but because I love her and want to spend the rest of my life with her.

35

BECKA

I can't believe I'm even considering this. It's crazy. It's insane.

And yet…

I want to do it. I want to say yes and marry this man today. I want to be wild and reckless and do something just for me without thinking about anyone else for once in my life. I know my family might be upset, but we can hold a big reception to celebrate with them later.

This would just be about me and Trent.

Why can't we get married today? I love him, he loves me. I trust him, more than I've ever trusted anyone, and I'm already committed to him. Why not make it official?

"Okay."

His eyes widen, and his mouth twitches like he's fighting back a smile. "Okay? Like, okay, you'll marry me today?" He sounds giddy which only makes me more confident in my answer.

"I'll marry you today."

He moves quickly until his lips are brushing against mine, and he's kissing me like he owns me, which I guess he does.

"I want Elise there."

He nods his head, like he was expecting me to say that. "And I want to go out and buy a white dress."

"Okay. I'll organize everything else with the hotel concierge, and we'll have a sunset wedding."

He gives me a dazzling smile, and from the strain on my cheeks I can tell that it matches my own. We're crazy, but at least we're crazy together.

"You're what?" Elise shrieks.

"I'm getting married. Tonight."

"Are you insane?"

"Possibly. I mean, this is crazy, right?"

"Uh, yeah!" she says, looking at me like I've grown three heads.

I pace back and forth in front of where she sits on the edge of her bed, her jaw hanging open and her eyes wide. "This is totally unlike me, but it also feels right, ya know?"

"No, I don't because this is crazy!"

I stop my pacing and grab her hands. "I love him. I love him so much more than I ever knew was possible, and I know I want to spend the rest of my life with him, so why wait? Why do we have to do what's socially acceptable and wait a specified amount of time before officially starting our lives together? Why can't we just decide and jump?"

Her mouth opens and closes several times before her shoulders drop. "You're right."

"I am?" I say, surprised she agreed with me so easily with how opposed she seemed to this only a few minutes ago.

She nods. "If you're sure. You have to be sure though. Marriage is a big deal."

"I know it's a big deal, and I'm one hundred percent sure."

She nibbles her lip like she's nervous, her eyes darting down to the carpet and then back to me before she finally steadies her gaze and asks softly. "This isn't because of what happened today with Dad, is it? This isn't some knee-jerk reaction to avoid dealing with the fact that our father turned out to be an even bigger asshole than we already suspected?"

I sit down next to her. "I'll admit seeing him today has probably had some impact on my decision, but mainly because he helped me see that a lot of things I've been blaming myself for all my life were never my fault. His leaving wasn't my fault. Seeing Dad gave me answers that I didn't completely know I'd been looking for. So part of this is definitely from seeing him, but it's not a knee-jerk reaction. I've known Trent most of my life, and when our friendship started back up again, it felt like no time had passed from when we'd been friends before. We clicked, instantly. It was like we were meant to find each other that day and be in each other's lives. We might've messed it up for a while, but that time apart showed us what the other person really means to us—at least it did for me, and based on things Trent's said, it did the same for him.

"We know what it's like to live without the other person, and we don't want that. I'm sure, El. I've never been surer of anything in my entire life. Am I scared? A little, yeah. I know we're going to face roadblocks and have highs and lows, but there's no one else I want to figure those things out with than him. I love him. And I'm marrying him tonight, with or without your blessing, but I'd rather have it and have you there to support us."

Elise tilts her head until it rests on my shoulder. "Of course, I support you. I still think you're a little crazy, but if you're sure and you're happy, then you know I'll be there."

A weight lifts from my shoulders knowing I have my sister's support. I wasn't lying when I said I'd still marry him without her blessing, but it would've hurt to not have her there. To not have at least one member of my family present when I marry the love of my life.

She lets out a chuckle.

"What?" I ask.

"Nothing, this is just a very rock star thing for Trent to do. The tabloids are gonna go crazy."

"Yeah, I'm trying not to think about that."

"You know you're going to have to deal with this for the rest of your life if you marry him, right? They're gonna follow you around and be all up in your business."

"I'm aware," I say with a heavy sigh. It's probably the one aspect of his life that I dislike the most. But I work in PR, and if anyone knows how to handle a situation, it's me.

"Anyway, on to more exciting things." I turn to my sister, a huge smile taking over my face. "You wanna help me pick out my wedding dress?"

The wedding is perfect, with beautiful soft lighting in a private garden ceremony that felt like Trent and I had found our own personal Garden of Eden. Afterward, we went out for drinks and celebratory dessert with Elise before going up to our hotel suite and having the most perfect night of wedded bliss any man or woman has ever had.

The bright sunlight filtering through our room the next morning wakes me up before Trent. So, I take it upon myself to wake him up with a very indecent good morning kiss.

"Fuckkk, Becka," he groans as I take his stiffening cock inside my warm, wet mouth. I let it go with a pop and smile at him seductively.

"That's Mrs. Bridger to you."

His eyes smolder, and he grabs my head and pulls me up his body until our mouths mold together in a kiss that leaves us both breathless and hungry for more. We take our pleasure in each other, each rough thrust of his cock inside my body making my toes curl as pleasure swirls deliciously inside me. It doesn't take us long to find our release together, and there's something about being husband and wife that makes it feel sweeter and stronger when we do.

We shower and dress, and then noticing the time, say a quick goodbye to Elise and make a mad dash to the airport so we don't miss our flight back to LA.

Time to face the music and break the news to the band.

36

TRENT

The return flight to LA goes by quickly. It feels like as soon as we get up in the air, we're already making our descent into LAX. Becka's hand is held securely in mine as we make our way to the car waiting for us. I'm confident in my decision to marry her, but I won't lie, I'm worried about how Tristan will take the news that I got married without him there. It's not like me to do something quite as rash as this, but I still have no regrets.

When we arrive at my house, he's sitting on the couch, his guitar in hand and a notebook and pen next to him. He glances up.

"Hey, how'd it go?"

Becka and I glance at each other before I decide to just rip off the Band-Aid. "Becka and I got married."

His eyes widen slightly, but he doesn't say anything, just continues to stare at me like he's trying to determine if I'm messing with him or not. Finally, after what feels like several long minutes, he gently places his guitar next to him and walks over to us. He gives Becka a hug first.

"Congratulations."

"Thank you," she says, a delicate pink blush spreading across her cheeks. She turns to me, "I need to run home and get some things. You still want me to stay here tonight with you?"

"Definitely. Nothing will keep me from my wife tonight." I love calling her that. It feels so perfect for her, like she was always meant to be mine. "If you want to stay at your place, I can grab a change of clothes and come with you."

"No. This is fine. It'll give you two some time together," she says with a brief glance at my brother.

"Sounds good." I give her a kiss that's soft and sweet but full of promises of much dirtier things to come later and then watch her get into the car before it pulls away. When I look back at my brother, he's staring at me again, his expression unreadable.

"Tris? You okay?"

"You really got married?"

I nod, holding up my left hand with my titanium wedding band on my ring finger as proof. "I didn't want to wait. I thought you of all people would understand."

His mouth turns down, and his eyes get that faraway haunted look that they sometimes get when I know he's thinking about the first time he met Jolie. "I understand." He wraps one arm around my shoulders and pulls me in for a hug. "I'm happy for you."

"Thanks, man."

We get the rest of the band and Robbie and Jolie on a conference call where I announce the news to them. They all take it way better than I expected, and Robbie immediately starts planning press releases. Kasen and Miles tease me about being shackled to the "ol' ball and chain," but then offer me sincere congrats.

But it's when Becka comes back to my house with a bunch of her stuff that I finally feel like everything in my life is exactly as it should be.

No longer do I feel lonely or lost. No, Becka found me and saved me and for that I plan to spend the rest of my life proving how grateful I am that no other man realized the gift they had in front of them.

"So, what do you think of this one?" Becka asks me as we lie in my plush California king bed. I glance at the venue she's pulled up on her laptop screen as we plan our wedding reception. Her family was happy for us, but her mom wanted a reception as soon as possible so she could celebrate with us properly.

So now we're trying to plan everything in less than a month. I've hired one of the best wedding planners I could find, but there are still a lot more decisions we have to make than I was expecting. Venue, flowers, colors, cake, guest list, sit-down dinner or just appetizers, and the list goes on.

But I'm determined to give Becka her dream wedding reception. After all, she's already made all of my dreams come true.

"I like it, and it fits all our criteria."

She smiles, her eyes lighting up as she scans through the slideshow of pictures showing different setups and décor that the venue can provide in-house.

"It'll hold all our family and friends and cater the dinner. They also have a florist that they work with that is available to do all the flowers, and they just had a cancellation, which means they can fit us in for two weeks from Saturday."

My gaze traces the lines of her face, watching her light up while she talks, and my heart feels lighter in my chest than I think it's ever felt.

This is what true happiness feels like.

"Then let's do it."

She turns to me, "Are you sure? Is there anything else you want?"

I lean toward her until her lips are just a whisper from mine. "All I want is you. Everything else is just extra."

EPILOGUE

Miles

My leg bounces in my chair while I sit listening to Trent record the same lyrics he's been recording for the last three hours. My head rests in my hand as I lean my elbow on the arm of the chair and try not to fall asleep. We've been working our asses off on this new album, and the long hours and lack of sleep is finally catching up with me.

Ned, our sound tech, stops recording and turns to Decker Cross, the biggest producer in LA and the man who's about to make this album our best yet. When Robbie told us Decker had shown an interest in working with us, I think we all thought he was fucking with us. Decker only works with Grammy-award-winning and Billboard chart-topping artists. And while we hit one of those milestones, we have yet to get a Grammy.

But that might all change with Decker in our corner.

I thought we'd made it big before, but we've reached another level if we're working with the elite of the LA music scene. It's a humbling experience.

If only I was getting better sleep and could actually keep my damn eyes open today, then it would be even better.

Turning to Robbie, I whisper, "Dude, I gotta get some caffeine in me or I'm gonna fade fast."

He glances at Ned and Decker discussing the vocals. "There's a coffee shop halfway down the block." He hands me a ten-dollar bill and says, "Be back in twenty minutes, or I can't guarantee that Decker won't try to replace you."

I think he's only half kidding.

But I can barely keep my eyes open, and we're not even halfway through this session, so I snatch the ten from his hand and make my escape. The walk is fairly quick, and the fresh air helps wake me up a bit. But then the aroma of coffee beans hits my nose the second I walk in the door, and it's like I can already feel the caffeine jolt.

Whoever invented coffee is my god. It's the life-sustaining force that keeps me going when we have long recording sessions like we've currently been doing. Making my way to the counter, I stand behind a woman with light brown hair wearing a black tank top and purple skinny jeans. But it's not her outfit that catches my attention, but the tattoos on her shoulder and upper arm. She places her order, and it's her voice that hits me next. The melodic rhythm of the way she talks makes me want to listen to her for hours.

I've always had a weird thing about voices. Just add it to the long list of "weird" things I'm into. But weird is subjective. It's all normal to me.

She finishes placing her order, pays, and then walks over to the pickup counter. I fight the urge to watch her walk away and instead step forward and place my own order, keeping in mind that I'm on a time crunch.

She's still waiting for her drink—or drinks as it appears—when I make my way over to the pickup counter to wait on my own drink, and I am suddenly grateful I've never liked drip coffee.

Unlike other people, she doesn't stare at her phone to waste time while she waits. Instead, she sticks her hands in her back pockets, her elbows bent, her body language open and relaxed. She intrigues me, but I've learned from personal experience never to judge a book by its cover. Too many times, people saw my long hair and laid-back personality and assumed I was some stoner drummer.

While I do occasionally smoke weed, that's not my drug of choice. No, it's always been the high I get from a sexual release that I've sought after—the kinkier the better.

"A vanilla latte and cappuccino," the barista calls out, and the brunette walks forward and grabs the two drinks.

"Thanks so much," she says in that sweet voice that makes my gut clench in the best way.

She walks over to the condiment bar to add cream and sugar to one of her drinks, and I fight the urge to bounce on my feet to dispel the nervous energy suddenly coursing through me. I want an excuse to talk to her, but I can see my window of opportunity closing fast. I just need one chance.

"A six shot Americano," the barista calls out, and I pounce on the chance to grab my drink and make my way over to where the brunette is still fixing her coffee.

I normally know what to say or what move to make when I'm about to flirt with a woman, but this one has me all kinds of twisted, and I can't figure out why.

"Excuse me," I say as I step next to her and grab a sugar packet from the holder in front of her.

"Oh sorry, I'm totally hogging the space," she says as she moves a step away from me, making room for me to put my drink on the counter while I doctor it with cream and sugar. She places the lid back on her coffee, and I know I'm about to lose my chance.

"I'm Miles," I say, smiling at her with my most winning smile.

Her eyes sparkle with what looks like amusement, which is not the reaction I was expecting. "I know," she says before walking away.

She's out the door before my brain catches up with her movements. *She knew who I was?* How is that possible? She didn't steal glances at me—I would've known since I was stealing plenty of glances at her.

Thrown off and uncharacteristically disappointed, I put the lid back on my coffee and walk back to the studio. I'm dangerously close to hitting that twenty-minute mark. I make my way to our recording booth, still processing my interaction with coffee girl and why I was so thrown off my game.

When I walk into the studio, I freeze, my eyes not convinced what I'm seeing isn't a figment of my imagination. But no, coffee girl is standing next to Decker, the second coffee she got at the shop now in his hand.

"Miles, glad you could make it back in time. If I'd known where you were off to, I could've told you to save yourself some time. Tamsin was picking up my usual for me."

"Tamsin?" I ask, my eyes bouncing back and forth between him and the woman that's captured my attention since the moment I saw her.

"My daughter," Decker says, taking a sip of his coffee and turning back to the board.

His...what now?

Fuck me.

Miles and Tamsin get their own story in Forbidden Intent, out now! Get 25% off when you buy it directly from my store. Use code: FI25

Keep reading for TWO bonus epilogues featuring Trent and Becka!

Follow or subscribe to my Ream page (https://reamstories.com/cadencekeys) and get exclusive sneak peeks and more!

BONUS EPILOGUE #1

Becka

Oh shit. Oh shit. Oh. Shit!

I stare at the screen of my phone in horror as notification after notification pops up from social media and the Google alerts that I set up when Trent and I first started dating. I knew this moment was inevitable, but I really hoped we'd have a little more time before the news broke.

Headlines bombard me one after the other, all announcing that Trent and I eloped.

One big problem.

I haven't told my family yet—apart from Elise since she was there and then promptly sworn to secrecy until I could tell Will, Lainey, and Mom myself.

Frantically, I close all the notifications and pull up my brother's number first since he's the one most likely to see media coverage before anyone else in my family.

Just when I think it's going to go to voicemail, he answers. "Hello?" he asks, his voice sounding slightly groggy, which makes sense.

"Uh, hey, so I need to tell you something. Something big."

He groans and then mumbles something unintelligible. "Right

now? It's six in the fucking morning, Becks. Can you call me back in a couple of hours?"

"No." I'm already relieved that there's no chance he's seen the news yet since he was obviously sleeping. I'm not willing to risk giving him more time to find out this news on his own.

"Fine. What's going on?" I love my brother, but he's definitely a grump when he hasn't had enough sleep.

I take a gulp of breath and place my hand on my chest in some weak attempt to steady my frantically beating heart. Here goes nothing.

"Trent and I got married."

Silence.

I'm not even sure I can hear him breathing, but then finally he says, "You what?!" There's no hint of grogginess in his voice now.

I close my eyes against the tone of shock in my brother's voice. "I got married. To Trent. In Vegas."

"I..." He huffs out a short laugh before it quickly morphs into him laughing hysterically.

Okay, that was not the reaction I was expecting. "Will?"

He takes a couple of deep breaths in an attempt to compose himself, and I wish desperately I could see him in person right now, because I can only imagine that his eyes are filled with mirth. "Have you told Mom yet?"

"Not yet, but I need to soon because Elise was there, and I know it's killing her to keep it from Mom."

"Oh man, this I gotta see. Do a family video call. This is going to be priceless," he says with one more laugh that leaves dread heavy in my gut. I had hoped I could quietly tell all my family, not tell them all at once on some FaceTime call.

I'm especially worried about how my mom is going to take it. I'm the first one to get married, and I didn't even give her a heads-up before I did it. Is she going to be hurt that I kept it from her? Or more upset that I didn't wait to have a big, elaborate wedding where she would be invited?

Nibbling my lip, I let out a heavy sigh. Time to face the music.

One by one, each member of my family joins our FaceTime call. Elise's face lights up with a huge smile. She's an open book, and it's a freaking miracle that she's kept this a secret at all.

Will's facial expression is exactly how I imagined it when we talked on the phone earlier. His eyes are tired, but there's an almost smug amusement on his face that makes me wish I could punch him in the arm. Lainey looks confused about why we're having a call at six in the morning, and my mom looks thrilled to see all her babies together, even if it is virtual. We don't get to FaceTime as a whole family very often given how crazy our schedules are.

My mouth opens to let the words out, but before I ever have a chance to speak, I hear footsteps behind me and turn just in time to see Trent walk out of the bathroom with a white towel wrapped low around his hips and one covering his head as he dries his hair.

The towel barely muffles the words that travel clearly across the room when he says, "Good morning, my gorgeous wife."

Gaping, I frantically turn back to my phone in time to see Lainey spit out her coffee, my mom's eyes widen, Elise giggle, and Will practically fall over from laughing so hard.

"His what?" my mom and Lainey both say at nearly the same time.

"Uh...yeah, so that's what I needed to tell you." I paste the most awkward smile on my face because this is so not going how I planned. "Surprise!"

I glance back at Trent who's now frozen in place, his own eyes wide and his mouth open. "Oh shit," he whispers. "Sorry."

I shrug it off even though this whole morning has gone to shit. He was in the shower when the alerts started rolling in. There was no way he could've known what he was walking in on.

"So, uh, yeah. Just wanted to let you know before the news got to you. It broke this morning and is now trending all over social media, and I didn't want you to find out that way."

"Wait, so you actually went and got married?" Lainey asks.

"When, how, where?" I can't tell if her tone is just surprised or if there's some hurt buried underneath that she wasn't there when it happened.

"It was a spur-of-the-moment thing in Vegas. Trent asked me to marry him and I said yes. Neither of us wanted to wait. So we didn't."

"Vegas? Elise, did you know about this?" my mom asks her, and there's definitely a little bit of hurt in her tone.

Elise winces. "Yeah, I did. Becka swore me to secrecy."

"So this only happened…what? Yesterday?" Lainey asks.

I nod and nibble my lip before saying, "Yeah."

"Holy shit. I can't believe you're married," Lainey says softly as if the reality is finally settling in.

"We're planning to have a big reception with all of our family and friends at some point. We do want you to celebrate with us, but we didn't want to wait to be married. I love him," I say finally, my eyes focused on Mom. She's hardly said a word, and I'm starting to get worried. I don't regret my choice to elope, but I do want her blessing.

"Well, for what it's worth, I think it's great," Will says, finally speaking up and easing the slight ache that's taken root in my chest.

"Me too," says Elise.

"Well, of course you would. You got to be there," replies Lainey, clearly a little salty that she wasn't invited, but I know I can smooth things over with her at our next brunch.

My mom, however, remains painfully silent.

"Mom," I say, my voice slightly cracking.

Trent's hand grazes my back as he sits down on the bed next to me, now fully clothed. The gesture is soothing, but it's when he takes my hand in his that I feel my strength being fortified. It's a reminder that we're in this together, and I don't have to face whatever comes alone.

We're partners—now and always.

My mom opens and closes her mouth several times before

she's finally able to get words out. "I'm…just surprised is all." She takes a deep breath and looks off screen like she's trying to think of the best way to frame her words. "It's a weird thing to be a mother. You hold these beautiful perfect babies in your arms, and you're both thrilled and terrified of what their future holds. It really is like having a piece of your heart living outside of your body. You want to protect them from any pain that comes their way while at the same time you want all their dreams to come true. It's hard when they get older and more independent because those wants and fears don't go away, but you also know they need to spread their wings and learn how to fly on their own. You start to feel a little helpless sometimes. I've seen you go through your fair share of heartbreak—even saw how hard it was on you when you and Trent weren't talking during his tour. I want the best for you, Becka. Always. I love you no matter what, and ultimately, I trust your decision. I just want to make sure that you're sure. Marriage is a big deal."

"I know it's a big deal, Mom. And it's not a decision I took lightly." I glance at Trent. "Neither of us did. We know it's not always going to be easy, but we're committed to each other."

Silence fills the air like a heavy weight on my chest, and it becomes hard to breathe as I wait for what she'll say next.

Her face breaks out in a big smile, and all my fear and anxiety immediately dissipates. "I'm so happy for you, Becka. And I can't wait to celebrate with you both whenever you have the reception. Let me know if there's any way I can help."

My face breaks out in a grin. "I will. Thank you, Mom."

"Of course, my sweet girl. Oh and Trent?"

"Yes, ma'am?"

"If you hurt my daughter, I will personally fly out to LA and rip you a new one."

Trent huffs out a laugh. "I would expect no less, but I can assure you, hurting Becka is the last thing I ever want to do."

He looks at me then, and my breath catches in my chest that this gorgeous, wonderful, and patient man is all mine.

"Well, I hate to break this up, but I have to start getting ready for work," says Lainey. "Becka, I'll see you at brunch next weekend?"

"Yeah, see you then," I say, relieved she doesn't seem as upset as she was earlier.

"I should get going too. I've got early workouts," says Will before he offers a goodbye to all of us and disconnects from the call.

Elise is next, and then my mom follows shortly after with one last congratulations to us.

I set my phone down on the bed and lean my head against Trent's shoulder, my whole body sagging against him in relief.

"Well, that could've gone better, but it turned out okay in the end."

"Yeah, I think so too. For a second there, I thought your mom was going to come through the phone and slap me upside the head."

I let out a laugh at the image that evokes, but don't move my head from where it rests against him. He feels so good and solid, in more ways than one.

"I love you," I say softly, wishing those words could adequately describe all that I feel for him, but they never seem strong enough.

He tilts my head up with his hand gently cupping my cheek. "Becka, I love you more than anything or anyone in this world. You're everything to me."

The heat that only Trent inspires spreads like a slow wildfire throughout my body until all I want to do is show him how much he means to me with every ounce of my body.

Reaching up, I grip the back of his neck and bring his mouth down to mine until our lips mold together and our tongues tangle in their familiar dance.

He strips me from my clothes slowly, like he's unwrapping a gift that he wants to savor, and it only makes my body burn hotter for him.

My hands roam across his chest, feeling the muscles flex underneath my fingertips. I slide my hands down to the hem of his shirt and then underneath, raising his shirt in the process inch by delicious inch. Helping me out, he reaches behind his neck and tugs his shirt up and over his head until it drops on the floor and his bare upper body is on full display.

I lick my lips, anticipation filling my gut because I know all the pleasure he can wring from me with that spectacular body of his, and suddenly I don't want to go slow. My eyes must give away my intent because he holds my face until my gaze meets his.

"Not today, baby. Today I'm going to savor every inch of you. We can go fast and furious tomorrow, but I don't have to leave for a few hours, and I plan to use every minute I can to make love to you until your body can't take the pleasure anymore."

My toes curl involuntarily, and I let out a shaky breath before nodding and leaning forward, capturing his lips in a heated kiss.

Trent makes good on his promise, taking me to heights I never knew existed. People always say sex tapers off when you're married—and maybe it will someday—but that day is most certainly not today. Something about being married has made the sex hotter, better. Every touch, every lick, every thrust takes me closer to another explosive orgasm until I'm a trembling, satisfied mess next to my husband.

When I turn to him—both of our bodies completely wrung out from our morning activities—he's got a blissful smile on his face. His eyes are filled with so much love that it takes whatever breath was left in my lungs away instantly.

"What did I ever do to deserve you?" I whisper.

He rolls toward me, his hand making a slow ascent up my body until he tucks a lock of sweaty hair behind my ear. "You were you, Becka. That's all. That's more than enough. I'm the one who asks myself every day what I did to deserve *you*."

Speechless—both from sex and his declaration—I snuggle into the safety of his body, and his arms immediately wrap around me and hold me close. I breathe in deeply as peace settles deep inside me.

I know our days won't always be this easy, but I no longer doubt that we'll face whatever comes together.

Always.

BONUS EPILOGUE #2

TRENT

"Let's make a baby."

My wife stares at me as our toddler, Logan, chases the dog with giddy squeals, although "chase" might be generous. Harass is probably more accurate.

"We already have a baby," she says, pointing to our rambunctious son.

"Let's make another one." I bend over, my hands bracing on each side of her chair, trapping her as I lean down and kiss her neck. "If Logan's left as an only child, he might turn into a little asshole, and we definitely can't have that." I kiss the other side of her neck. "Plus, Teddy needs another cousin."

"Oh, does he now?" she says, but there's a smile on her gorgeous face, and her eyes have that heated look that always makes my heart beat a little faster.

Some days I still can't believe this woman is mine. It's not always easy, but nothing worth it ever is. And even on our worst days, I know she has my back just like I have hers. We're a team, always.

"Daddy!" squealed loudly behind me is my only warning before a head rams between my legs, and I grunt as I drop my forehead to Becka's shoulder and squeeze my hands on the armrests so I don't fall on top of her from the crippling pain.

"Well, we may not be having any more kids now," I groan.

I love that kid with all my heart, but goddamn, he's the biggest cockblocker.

Becka giggles uncontrollably and bites her lip as she tries—and fails—to control her laughter. "Apparently Logan isn't ready for a sibling."

"How about Mommy?" I murmur, trying to ignore the pain still throbbing between my legs from my kid's impeccable aim.

She shakes her head, but her smile spreads wide across her face. She glances over at her phone sitting on the small table next to her chair, checking the time. "Mommy thinks it's time for my little guy to go down for his nap," she says gently, moving me aside and picking up our son, who giggles and squeals in his mom's arms as she tickles him. When she stops, he takes a big breath and then wraps his arms around her neck and drops his head to her shoulder, a content little smile on his face.

My heart feels so full in my chest, I sometimes wonder if it could actually burst. Becka's such an amazing mom, even if she doubts herself sometimes. She's the kind of mom I always wished I had, and I get great satisfaction knowing my son will never have to go through what I did as a child.

She turns to me. "And once he's down, then maybe Daddy will get his answer."

Whatever pain was still lingering in my southern region immediately evaporates. It's been days since I've had quality alone time with my wife. Kids are a blessing—no doubt about it—but it's also hard to find time for each other when we have such a helpless little person relying on us for all his needs. He also seems determined to do any activity that could pose a risk to his safety—putting everything not nailed down in his mouth, climbing fucking *everything*. I swear to God, my kid was a monkey in another life and he's trying to send me to an early grave. Three-year-olds are daredevils, and he's not graceful about it. The kid will trip over air while running down the hallway after our dog.

And yet, I still want another one. I'd fill our whole fucking house with kids if Becka would let me. She teases me that I have a breeder kink because I found her irresistible while she was pregnant. Truthfully, I find her irresistible no matter what. As far as I'm concerned, I won the fucking lottery when Becka married me. Adding kids to the mix is just the cherry on top.

I follow her to Logan's room where she changes his diaper—because he's not quite ready for full-on potty training—engaging in conversation with him the entire time and making me smile from how cute they are together. He's such a mama's boy, but I can't blame him.

She puts him in his bed, covering him with his blanket, and he immediately rolls to his side and closes his eyes. One thing he inherited from Becka that I'll always be grateful for is the ability to fall asleep quickly. When he's tired, he goes down no problem. I've been warned that a second kid will likely not be anywhere close to as easy as he's been in this regard, but I'm willing to take that risk.

Differences are healthy, and I'm up for a challenge.

Now that we all have families, we decided to only tour every two to three years, which has been great. Our tour last year was our best yet, especially after the success of our latest album. Tristan's songs are better than ever, and as much as the label was worried about how our popularity would diminish once we all settled down, it's surprisingly been the opposite. Our record sales are higher than ever. We were on the cover of *Rolling Stone* a few months ago, and our last single stayed on the *Billboard* Top 10 for five months—even becoming a viral sound on social media. But none of that success compares to these moments of watching my wife and son together, of being home with them.

Of building a family with the woman of my dreams.

Becka closes the door softly and then spins around to face me, her wicked smile teasing me with what's to come if her heated gaze is any indication. She rubs her hands up my chest until they circle my neck and then she leans against my body. My arms instantly wrap around her, holding her close so she can feel how hard I already am for her.

"So, do you want to try for another boy or a girl this time?"

I give her my most devilish smile as I say, "Both. Definitely both."

Did you know Will and Gina have their own book? Read Across the Middle today! Or start the LA Wolves series for FREE with In the Grasp

AFTERWORD

I honestly wasn't sure I would get this book done in time. I wrote the first draft in less than three weeks in July. It's the fastest book I've ever written, probably because the characters had been screaming at me for several months already. The words flowed and I the characters came to life. I felt confident that I could probably even write book 2 before the end of summer—or at least get it started.

Then I found out I was pregnant, and less than a week later I was hit with HORRIBLE morning sickness—although, let's be real, it was all day sickness.

Nothing I tried that had worked in my previous pregnancy worked. By the end of August, I was put on meds that worked, but the side effect was that they totally wiped me out. In a blink, September passed me by and then mid October before I felt somewhat human. By then, I was down to the wire on getting re-writes done for In the Grasp, a project I'd promised readers I'd release to them in early December.

So Noble Intent got put on the back burner until after Thanksgiving. Then, it was a frantic push to get it through multiple rounds with my editors so it would be ready for release in time. I can't even begin to tell you how incredible my editors, Ann Suh and Ann Riza, are. I'm forever thankful that I found them (and a HUGE thank you Claire Hastings for sending me their way). I could not have finished this book in time without them.

I also need to thank my mom for watching my son when my husband had to work and I was frantically trying to reach my deadlines. Also, for all the help she did around the house so I wouldn't lose my mind.

To Daphne, Kenna, Kelly, and Ellie: Thank you for your constant encouragement and support and being the best writing tribe a girl could ask for. I'm so thankful we found each other.

To Kate Farlow for once again designing a beautiful cover and making my vision come to life.

To Lindee Robinson for your incredible photography skills.

To my best friend, Rikki, for always supporting me and being a sounding board (whether it's about writing or life). Best part of studying abroad was meeting you.

To my husband for your constant love and support, and to my son and unborn daughter for being the miracles that made me believe anything was truly possible.

And last, but never least, to you for taking the time to read my books (especially if you made it all the way to the end of this). Thank you for supporting me. You've made my dreams come true and I'm so incredibly thankful for you.

ABOUT THE AUTHOR

Cadence Keys is a bestselling steamy romance author. When she's not coming up with plots for her books, she's chasing her rambunctious toddlers around or cuddling with her husband. She loves writing heartfelt stories with relatable characters and a guaranteed happily ever after.

Learn more about her and her books on her website: www.cadencekeysauthor.com

- facebook.com/cadencekeysauthor
- x.com/cadencewrites
- instagram.com/cadencekeysauthor
- bookbub.com/profile/cadence-keys
- goodreads.com/cadencekeysauthor
- tiktok.com/@cadencekeysauthor

ALSO BY CADENCE KEYS

LA WOLVES FOOTBALL SERIES

In the Grasp

Across the Middle

Down by Contact

Taking the Handoff

Defending the Backfield

After the Snap

RAPTUROUS INTENT ROCKSTAR SERIES

Noble Intent

Forbidden Intent

Devoted Intent

Promised Intent

BREAKING THE RULES SERIES

Only a Kiss

Just for Tonight

Made in the USA
Columbia, SC
24 August 2024